PRAISE FOR RAY OKON SERIES

Praise for Under The Radar
As current as today's headlines...
Nigeria is at the brink of a state of emergency, as an alarming number of the deaths across the country churns in a fortnight. But DSS Agent Ray Okon suspects something sinister as the incidences all have similar patterns.

Under The Radar is a sophisticated fast-paced crime thriller novel set in Nigeria, riddled with mysteries and intrigues as our favourite DSS Agent Ray Okon is back, to battle with formidable forces and unravel the mysteries behind these deaths.

I enjoyed this book because of its relevance to current happenings, the action, the romance, and the police procedurals. Also, I love the fact that several Nigerian cities were featured, giving readers the rich flavour from our diverse cultural backgrounds.

I rate this book 5 stars.
Edidiong Esshiet
Author of The Lagos Swap

I remember reading 'Ties that Bind' and thinking it doesn't get better than this. Well, little did I know that following fast on its heels is this phenomenal masterpiece 'Under the Radar.'

Having fallen in love with the sensible and dedicated Ray Okon in 'Ties that Bind,' I could not help but root for him throughout this book. I feared for his life at several times. And that of the dazzling Sarah Aderinsola. They were a match made perfect by the security and intelligence agencies.

Stanley Umezulike has weaved a powerful story about deep seated crime in an almost dysfunctional society, a story that sent chills down my body as it did Ray and his team. A story that had me at the edge of my seat almost saying out loud, "what next?"

Like its predecessor, 'Under the Rader' is a book you cannot put down till the last page. You will actually release the breath you weren't aware of holding. Fast paced, delicious and simple of diction. I highly recommend this book to readers anywhere in the world.

Stanley Umezulike shines again.

--- Christiana Agboni, author of Yuletide Sparks

Ray Okon faces a challenging criminal investigation at first thought to be an open-and-shut case. The more he delves into solving it, the deeper he digs into the corrupt world of the upper echelon in Nigeria. The setting is modern-day Nigeria, and the reader experience life through the images the author paints with words.

The main character, Ray Okon, is well-developed with human frailty and internal and external challenges he must face. Ray is realistic and connecting with him and sharing his journey was easy.

I received a complimentary ARC copy of Stanley Umezulike's Under the Radar and found it to be a page-turner packed with action. The plot is well defined and easy to follow, with many twists and turns, a true crime mystery.

--- Leila Kirkconnell, author of Missing

Under The RADAR

A Ray Okon Crime Thriller

STANLEY UMEZULIKE

First Published in Great Britain in 2022 by
LOVE AFRICA PRESS
103 Reaver House, 12 East Street, Epsom KT17 1HX
www.loveafricapress.com

LOVE AFRICA
PRESS
African Love Stories

ISBN: 978-1-914226-27-4
Also available as eBook

DEDICATION

To my friend and brother, Louis Akwaeze. Thank you for helping me bring Ray Okon series to life.

ACKNOWLEDGEMENTS

My deepest gratitude goes to the Almighty God, to Him be all the glory.

Throughout the writing of this book, I've had a great team cheering me on, offering advice and providing me with the support I needed to keep moving forward.

I'm grateful to my brother, friend and business partner, Louis Akwaeze, who helped me create a writing schedule that enabled me to write four times every week and still be able to do my work at the office.

My special thanks goes to my great friends, Christiana Agboni. Thank you for your invaluable input and support at every step of the process.

Major thanks to my wonderful author friends, Precious Osikha, Uduakobong Eshiet, Tracey Fletcher, Diana Silvia, Leila Kirkconnell, and Obinna Kelechi Obioma, who were my support system while I was working on this story.

To my mentor, Victoria Sanford, I'm grateful for your encouragement. Thank you for helping me take a bold step in my writing career.

I'm also grateful to my friend and amazing writer, Ijeoma Mbah, a graduate of the University of Ibadan in Nigeria, who helped me during my research especially when I was writing a scene set in the city of Ibadan.

I owe a huge debt of gratitude to my family. I'm grateful for your support.

I'm grateful to all the members of Prolific Fiction Writers Community. You are the best.

Finally, my deepest thanks go to my publisher, Love Africa Press. Thank you for helping to make this dream come true. I'm grateful to all those who helped to bring this book to life. Thank you so much.

BLURB

Some cases will get you killed

When the body of a final-year student at the University of Lagos is found in the lagoon, the police rule it an open and shut case: suicide. But as the bodies of more final-year university students end up in the lagoon, DSS Special Agent Ray Okon is called to investigate the incidents sending chills across the country.

National Intelligence Agency security expert Sarah Aderinsola is investigating a similar case. Ray and the DSS Criminal Investigation Department team up with her to find answers.

As Ray and Sarah race across university campuses and peel layers of deceit, they face a terrible evil residing under the radar, unnoticed — until now. Worse, it is ready to shatter the fragile heart of the nation.

To save the country, they must risk their lives to stop a ruthless enemy determined to bring the nation to its knees.

CHAPTER ONE

Third Mainland Bridge, Lagos

The girl lay on the roadside. Her clothes were stinking wet. Two Federal Road Safety Corps members had pulled her corpse out of the lagoon an hour earlier. Sadness clouded her sunken eyes and swollen face.

Ray Okon, a special agent from the Department of State Services (DSS), pulled on his gloves, observed her body closer, and shivered. He was with Doctor Kenneth Akingbola, a pathologist from the DSS Criminal Investigation Department. Beside him stood Inspector James Ibru, from the Lagos State Police Headquarters, whom they would be liaising with on the case.

Ray watched as the FRSC officer close to him removed a clump of dirt that clung to the corner of her mouth. Her mouth was partially open. Her body had started to decompose. The smell of death surrounded the whole place, making him want to vomit. Even after being in homicide for a long time, he could not get used to the stench.

Dark clouds covered the sky. Nearby, a strange insect chirped one last time. It was six on Tuesday morning in the first week of October. Ray remembered how he felt when he woke up that morning. Was it because of his nightmares? It was as if the day brought evil with it.

The phone call that interrupted his sleep had given him the unwelcome news. Just yesterday, he'd flown from Abuja to Lagos to consult with the Lagos Police in unravelling a case of suicide that had sent shockwaves across the country. Nonso Onyeama, a final year student at the University of Lagos, went to the Third Mainland Bridge and jumped into the lagoon three days ago after making a cryptic post on the popular social media platform, Kedochat.

The case became high-profile when the police discovered the twenty-two-year-old was the son of the deputy speaker of the House of Representatives, Honourable Badmus Onyeama. Soon, an order from DSS came asking Ray to join in solving the case. Ray, recently appointed as the director of operations at DSS' CID, was sent to Lagos by his superiors to join the police in the investigation.

What troubled Ray was that the university was his alma mater. He'd been thinking about the case since he heard the tragic news. This morning, he'd received a call that they found another dead body in the same lagoon at the Third Mainland Bridge.

Ray turned to face the police officer beside him. "Inspector, can you briefly tell me what happened here? What's her name?"

"Her name is Ifeoluwa Oladipo. She is the niece of Senator David Adebayo. She was a final year student at the University of Lagos, where she was studying Linguistics," Inspector James said.

Lines of worry creased Ray's temple. *Another final-year student.*

"Two days ago, she came to this bridge and jumped inside the Lagoon," the inspector continued. "We received a call yesterday evening from her distraught mother who told us they had been searching for her. We started retracing her steps. This morning, FRSC officers pulled her body out of the lagoon and informed us about the incident. We called you the moment we received the news."

"How do we know this is suicide?" Ray asked.

"She left a post on her Kedochat profile two days ago," Inspector James replied.

Ray held his gaze. "Please, let me see it."

The inspector lifted a Samsung smartphone, opened the Kedochat App, and searched for her name. He gave the phone to Ray ten seconds later.

Ray narrowed his eyes as he read the brief post she left on her Kedochat timeline:

I'm tired, mum. School is tough. Let me go home, please.

The message had about two thousand comments. *This is strange.*

Ray returned the smartphone to the officer. "What do the police make out of this?" he asked.

"At first, her Kedochat post wasn't clear. If you look at the first fifty comments in her post, you will discover that they assumed that what she meant by going home was that she wanted to go to her parents' house. But now that she is dead, it's clear that this is a case of suicide. She has gone home," Inspector James explained.

Ray looked away the moment the inspector finished speaking. Thinking about the girl's death made him feel sad.

"She is a final year student going through a lot of stress in school. It's unfortunate that she had to give up and end her life this way," the inspector said. His words hung in the air for a minute.

Inspector James stepped out, saying he had to make a phone call. Ten minutes later, he came back and approached Ray. "Thank you, Ray, for coming to assist us at such short notice. If you will excuse me, I'd like to go and write a report I'll give to my superiors. We will inform her family about the sad news and bring a vehicle to return her body to her parents after a routine autopsy check at the morgue."

Ray nodded and forced a smile as he watched him leave. He stared at the body a minute longer, and a tear trickled from the corner of his eyes. She looked young and twentyish. She was still at her ripe age. A young lady with her whole life ahead of her. She probably had dreams she wanted to achieve. Now, all of that had turned to dust.

His intense gaze settled on Doctor Kenneth's five-foot-nine frame. "Doctor, can you give me an estimate of the time of death?"

The tall, dark-skinned pathologist nodded and bent closer to observe the corpse. "Twenty-four to twenty-six hours at most. She may have died five minutes after jumping inside the lagoon."

Ray tightened his jaw. "Do we know anything else about her?"

"She has a boyfriend named Mark Ogundele," an FRSC agent beside him said. "Mark is the Student Union Deputy President at the University of Lagos."

"Thank you," Ray said to the agent. "I'll set up a meeting with him today."

"Doc?"

"Yes," the pathologist replied.

"Get me details of her funeral, including the location. I'd like to talk with members of her family," Ray said.

"Yes, sir. Will do."

Five minutes later, a police van stopped in front of them. Two muscular men came out of the vehicle. They covered her body with a white sheet, placed it on a stretcher, and put the corpse inside the van.

Ray couldn't imagine her family's pain at losing their daughter and was glad he didn't have to break the news to them. Instead, he would head back to his hotel room in Ikeja.

He entered the car Lagos Police assigned to him and started the engine. One question crawled into his mind. *What else is going on here?*

CHAPTER TWO

When Ray returned to his hotel room at Sheraton Hotel in Maryland, Ikeja, he changed into a white sleeveless Nike tank top and black shorts, took his headphone, and headed to the hotel gym.

"Good morning, Ray," Donald Odoh greeted him while flashing sparkling white teeth.

Donald was tall and slim with muscled arms. He was the guy the hotel employed to run the gym. Ray met him yesterday evening when he came down to use the treadmill.

"How are you, Donald?"

"Bubbling with energy."

Ray smiled. Both men shook hands, and Ray entered the gym. He saw three middle-aged men working out with dumbbells under the direction of a female gym instructor. A man in his mid-twenties grunted as he lifted a barbell.

When Ray got to the treadmill, he wore his headphone and gripped the front rail. *Big Energy* by LadiPoe started playing in his ears. He turned on the treadmill and jogged slowly while doing chest presses. He bent his arms, bringing his upper body close to the front rail and display panel, and then pushing himself back up.

He faced the rear of the treadmill, extended his arms, and took hold of the handrail. He did another set of chest presses using push-up motion. Next, he set the speed to 4 km/h, turned his back on the console and started walking backwards while the music banged in his ears.

I'm tired, mum. School is tough. Let me go home, please.

Ray's jaw tightened when an image of the dead girl with a swollen face flashed through his mind. He switched his position, turned to face the console, and started running. He watched the speed on the console as it moved gradually from four kilometres per hour to ten kilometres per hour. He maintained his pace when he got to fourteen kilometres per hour.

An hour later, he checked the time on his Rolex watch. It was 9 am. He stepped away from the treadmill and saw Donald as he approached him with a bottle of water.

"You need this," Donald said.

Ray collected it. "Thank you."

As he gulped down the bottle of water, sweat slipped from his cheek to his chest. He stared at his watch again and headed back to his hotel room. He would shower, eat breakfast and head to the University of Lagos.

***

At 11 am, Ray, Frank Igwe, and Inspector James Ibru went to see Mark Ogundele.

Frank had arrived from Abuja two hours earlier. Dark-skinned, strong on his feet, and of average height, he'd been Ray's partner at

Homicide and Anti-Drug Trafficking Unit in DSS Abuja Central Branch. Then, Ray was promoted and reassigned to the DSS Criminal Investigation Department as Director of Operations.

Before Ray travelled to Lagos, he'd requested that Frank should be added to DSS CID and assigned to this case. His superiors had approved, and now, he was glad that Frank had joined them.

James drove the police squad car while Ray and Frank sat in the back. Lagos was a bustling megacity of BRT Buses, yellow *molues*, loud hawkers and endless traffic jams. The sun shone brightly, illuminating the faces of pedestrians who rushed to appointments.

Surprisingly, traffic was light, and they arrived at Akoka Road thirty minutes later, passing through the massive gate of the University of Lagos. James turned into University Road. Nostalgia tinged Ray's lips with a bittersweet smile as their vehicle drove through well-tarred roads, past the House of Creativity, Founani Nigeria Limited, and the beautiful St Thomas Moore Catholic Chaplaincy building. Minutes later, they passed the Chapel of Our Light building and the University of Lagos Central Mosque.

The familiar roads and departmental buildings hit Ray with a wave of memories. This was his alma mater. He enjoyed his time as a student here. Hence, his determination to get to the root of this case.

With help from students, they found out Mark Ogundele would be at the Student Union building on the campus. He seemed to be a popular guy.

Outside the building, James sent a student to call Mark.

Three minutes later, a young man walked out, dressed in a striped T-shirt and black trousers. Tall, dark, with huge forearms, he looked to be in his early twenties and had a tattoo on his neck. He swaggered towards them. "Someone said you were looking for me?"

"Are you Mark Ogundele?" Ray asked.

"Yes. Who's asking?" the young man eyed them.

"I'm Detective James from the Lagos CID, and these are my colleagues from DSS CID." The officers flashed their badges. "We just want to ask you some questions about Ifeoluwa Oladipo. I believe you know we brought out her body from the Lagoon this morning."

Ray watched as the big boy on campus leaned his muscular body against the squad car and broke into tears. "Oh my God. Ifeoluwa. I still can't believe she's gone." He wiped his tears and continued to sob silently.

"She was your girlfriend, right?" Ray asked.

Mark nodded.

"Did you notice anything strange about her behaviour over the past few weeks?" Ray asked.

Mark shook his head. "No, Ifeoluwa is a bundle of energy. Full of life. She has many plans for her future and is always excited whenever she talks about them. She is hard-working and is top of the class in her Linguistics department."

He is still talking about her in the present tense. The love he has for her is evident in his eyes, Ray thought.

Frank stepped closer to him and asked, "When was the last time you saw her?"

"Three days ago. We both attended the cultural day event on Campus. We were together throughout that day. Unfortunately, that was the last day I saw and heard from her."

They kept asking him questions, but he continued to cry and said he knew nothing else about the case and could not think of any reason the love of his life would take her own life. His eyes were red, and he wasn't ashamed to cry even when other students who passed by saw what was going on and stood to watch.

When James asked to see his phone, Mark obliged and showed them the last message he had sent her three days earlier.

Ifeoluwa: *I love you, babe*.

She had also dropped a heart emoji.

Mark: *I will always love you, sweetheart*.

James scrolled through their recent WhatsApp chat messages. The three men saw nothing in the chats to indicate that the two lovebirds had any problems. When he closed the WhatsApp App, Ifeoluwa's picture filled the screen. James gave the smartphone back to Mark.

"Apart from you, who else is her close friend?" Ray asked.

Mark raised his face and said, "Annie Okeke. She is her roommate and best friend."

James allowed Mark to leave after dropping his card and getting Annie's address. They left five minutes later. When James pulled the car out of the university gate, he headed to the neighbourhood where Annie Okeke lived off-campus.

CHAPTER THREE

Abule Oja, the neighbourhood where Annie Okeke lived, was five minutes away from the University of Lagos gate. On their way, Inspector James got a call from the Lagos State Police Command. He stopped the car on University Road, where she lived, and Ray and Frank alighted from the vehicle.

"Thank you, agents. Keep me updated," he said to them.

They nodded, and he drove off.

As Ray walked through the streets, he observed his surroundings. Abule Oja was a residential area. It had gated houses where university students lived.

The place was a hub of small businesses that the students referred to as Akokites patronized. Beauty salons, skin care therapies, boutiques, and supermarkets lined both sides of the streets.

Ray and Frank walked fast and soon reached Victory lodge, the two-storey building where Annie had her apartment. Ray asked for direction from a girl who was washing clothes in the compound, and she told them that Annie's apartment was on the second floor.

Ray knocked when they reached Annie's front door. The door cracked open thirty seconds later, and the eyes of a frightened girl stared at them. She was dark, twentyish, and had a petite frame.

"Hi Annie, my name is Ray Okon. We are DSS agents." Ray showed her his badge. "We would like to ask you a few questions."

The girl looked at them with suspicion. Sadness clung at the corners of her eyes. Ray knew that losing her best friend would hit her hard.

She opened the door a minute later and allowed them to enter.

Annie lived in a one-room self-contained apartment. The room was neat and well arranged. Skincare lotions and makeup kits lined the corner of the windowsill. A flat-screen TV hung in the centre of the wall. A framed photograph on the wall caught Ray's eyes, and he stepped closer to it.

Frank joined Ray a moment later. It was a picture of Annie and Ifeoluwa—the two best friends. In the image, their smiles brightened their faces. The gowns they wore showed they took the photo at their matriculation ceremony. Then, four years later, one of them committed suicide. What went wrong?

As Frank went to observe another picture on the wall, Ray looked at Annie and said, "Annie, we are sorry for your loss. Losing a close friend is hard. From what I've observed, both of you are very close. Please, take heart."

The girl heard him and looked away. He saw the pain in her eyes when she glanced back at him.

"We've met her boyfriend, Mark. We just want to ask you a few questions about Ifeoluwa. She was your roommate, is that correct?"

The girl nodded.

"When was the last time you saw her?"

"She left here four days ago. I knew she was among the organizers of the cultural day event at the university. It kept her busy. She didn't tell me when she would be back. I wasn't worried about it until I heard the news ... Since then, I have received social media messages and calls from her friends. Most of them blamed me for not doing anything after seeing her Kedochat post. I could have stopped her from doing it if she had been here. I could have...." She began to cry, and they allowed her to mourn.

When she wiped her tears, Frank asked, "Did you notice anything strange about her behaviour in the past three months before she died?"

Annie shut her eyes and seemed to be thinking about the question. Finally, she opened them and said, "Ifeoluwa used to be so happy and lively in the past, but two months ago, she changed."

"What happened?" Ray asked.

Annie shook her head. "I don't really know. She kept to herself and refused to open up to me, which was strange considering that we were best friends. She was no longer the Ifeoluwa I knew. Something was eating her up. I guess that was why she committed suicide when she couldn't take it anymore."

Ray brought out a notepad and scribbled fast.

"Was she having any problem in school or at home?" Frank asked.

"I don't know. If she did, she never told me. She was top of the class and was on good terms with her family." She paused, then continued, "Everything about her death is strange."

"You never figured out what would have made her take her own life," Ray said.

The girl shook her head. "I felt she was hiding something from me, but I didn't know what it was."

They asked her more questions but couldn't get any other information from her.

As they were about to leave, Ray brought out his card. "Here's my card. If there is anything you remember, please don't hesitate to call me." He gave it to her.

"Ask Dele. She tells him everything."

They heard her voice and stopped.

Ray turned and faced her. "Who is Dele?"

"Dele is her elder brother," she replied.

Ray made a mental note to question Dele during Ifeoluwa's funeral.

As they stepped out of the building, a question clutched at the corner of his mind. *What did Ifeoluwa hide from her best friend?*

CHAPTER FOUR

Surulere, Lagos

"Ashes to ashes. The Lord giveth. Now, he has taken," the priest in white soutane and purple stole said as he held a shovel filled with sand and heaved it inside the grave.

When the dirt hit the casket with a thud, a woman in black started to cry. Two boys and a girl Ray figured were her children tried to console her but couldn't.

As she and her children took turns carrying the shovel and dropping sand inside the grave, the choir began to sing Amazing Grace.

After dropping sand with the shovel, Senator David Adebayo wiped his tears with a white handkerchief. The media had reported that the senator and his niece were close.

He went ahead and hugged the woman. She cried on his shoulder and stopped a minute later. Then, he led her and the children towards the one-storey building.

"She told me she wanted to be a teacher," Ifeoluwa's mother said between sobs as the senator led her into the building.

Ray, Frank, James, and a middle-aged police officer going bald at the front of his head stood in the thick of the mourning crowd, watching the funeral proceedings in the one-storey residential compound in Surulere. They had arrived thirty minutes earlier and joined family members and close friends who mourned the loss of Ifeoluwa Oladipo. Since then, they stood watch and functioned as security at the funeral ceremony.

Knowing the girl died at a youthful age made Ray's chest constrict. The men engaged in low conversations about the case, then went into the house twenty minutes later to console the family.

As he consoled the family, Ray learned their father died when Ifeoluwa was eleven. He didn't want to think of the pain the young girl would have felt at losing her father at such an early age.

He knew the terrible feeling. He'd lost his father when he was ten—a hit-and-run accident. Never arrested, the driver had vanished without a trace. The police dropped the case two years later, just like that. It was now a cold case, forgotten by the police and the public.

Ray grew up boiling with rage at the incident. But he managed to contain it. To put it correctly, the love of his life, Loretta Olawale, helped him put the lid on it.

They had met at the University of Lagos and had been close ever since. An incident drove them apart a year ago, but they found their way back to each other's arms. She lived in Abuja, the capital city. She had texted him that she would be coming to Lagos as part of her plan to open the branch office of her fashion house. Naturally, he couldn't wait to see her.

As he grew up, all those frustrations and pent-up anger motivated him to study criminal law and join the department of state services to fix the broken system. Finding and nailing the criminals who destroyed innocent lives was one of the two things that gave him peace of mind: that and his love, Loretta.

When Ray reached where the victim's mother was, he decided it was the wrong time to ask her questions about her daughter's death. The woman was in another world with sadness and pain covering her eyes. He introduced himself and his fellow officers and consoled her.

When they left the building, Senator David met them and asked about the case. "I'm aware my niece is not the first person to die this way," he said.

"The case is ongoing, sir," James said. "We will keep you updated."

As they walked to their squad car, Ray whispered to Frank. Frank nodded and went back to the house. He came to the vehicle with Dele twenty minutes later. Dele was dark, muscular, and of average height. He wore black like the others. Ray read his expression and saw a young man raging with anger.

Ray showed Dele his badge and explained who they were. After the brief introduction, he said, "Dele, we need your help. Your response may help us understand what is going on. Do you have an idea of what would have made your sister commit suicide?"

"Yes, I do. That son of a bitch is responsible for my sister's death," he said.

Ray and his colleagues became alert.

"Who?" Ray asked.

"Mark Ogundele."

Ifeoluwa's boyfriend, Ray thought. He exchanged glances with his colleagues.

"What did he do?" he asked.

Dele took a moment to calm his nerves. "My sister confided in me that she was pregnant. Her boyfriend, Mark Ogundele, refused to take responsibility for the pregnancy. She was afraid to tell mum, who ran the house with an iron rod. She aborted the baby, and the guilt crushed her. It's obvious that it propelled her to take her own life."

"When was this?"

"Six weeks ago."

Ray's eyes widened. He asked him more questions, and the three investigators left five minutes later.

Ray's phone rang as James drove the car out of the neighbourhood. He pulled it out from his pocket and stared at the screen. It was the pathologist, Dr Kenneth Akingbola.

"We've done the autopsy," the doctor said.

Ray put the phone on speaker. "What did you discover?"

"The autopsy revealed that she had an abortion. But that was not what killed her."

She jumped into the lagoon, Ray thought.

"Did you discover anything else?"

"None," he said, and the call ended.

Inspector James brought his phone to his ear and started making calls and issuing orders.

***

The police arrested Mark Ogundele two hours later. Ray and Frank were with them when it happened inside the University of Lagos main campus. Ray read his expression as they handcuffed him but only saw pleading in his eyes.

"Mark, let's ask you this question one last time," Frank said. "Were you both having problems in your relationship?"

"Yes, we were having problems in our relationship. That was when she told me that—"

James cut in. "That she was pregnant."

"Yes. I'm sorry I gave her money to remove the baby. That time was the worst period of my life. My head was full. I panicked. I wasn't thinking straight." He stared at them with tears in his eyes. "Please, I'm sorry. I swear it didn't lead her to commit suicide."

Mark kept blabbing as the police loaded him in a van and took him away.

Frank joined Ray in his Mercedes. Ray drove him back to his hotel before proceeding to his.

When Ray got to his room, he wondered if getting pregnant and aborting the baby were enough reasons for Ifeoluwa to make the Kedochat post and jump into the lagoon. That was what the police believed. But did it add up?

CHAPTER FIVE

The chilly wind whipped at Patrick Okoli's face, and he hurled off curses. He was driving a huge truck filled with building materials across the Third Mainland Bridge. The time was 4 am, and this part of Lagos had already started bustling with activities. He knew the bridge would soon become heavy with traffic. Here in Lagos, people woke up as early as 3 am to beat the notorious Lagos traffic and get to work on time.

Last week, Patrick failed to deliver goods on time because he got stuck in traffic for eight hours. His client refused to pay, claiming he'd lost money due to the delay. Patrick was determined to make sure the incident never happened again.

He had a wife and five children. All his kids were in school. The bills mounted. He had to be on the road daily to keep his family happy. He knew he was in a terrible rat race—one he would never escape. Some of his colleagues had died from the stress after spending many hours on the road. The pressure of the job of a Lagos truck driver was too much.

He peered into the road as he sped on, the yellow hues from the traffic gracing his sight. The road was clear. He heaved a sigh of relief. *This is rare in Lagos*, he thought.

If he delivered the goods on time, he would go back to his house and sleep well so that he could satisfy Natasha, his crazy mistress, at night in their hotel.

If his family's mounting bills did not take him to an early grave, his job or Natasha would give him a heart attack. Patrick knew this. There was nothing he could do about it.

His thick fingers tightened on the steering wheel when he saw a sharp bend at the last minute and swerved the vehicle fast to the other side. "Jesus Christ," he shouted and took a deep breath to calm down his racing heart.

His eyes were heavy with sleep. He hadn't been having enough rest. He was supposed to be on his bed sleeping but couldn't. Not when he only worked at night. He slowed down the truck and looked ahead. Soon, he would drive out of the bridge and be on his way to Ikeja, his delivery location. He was close.

At that moment, a reflection in the lagoon across the bridge caught his attention. The traffic light illuminated the object. *A massive fish*, he thought as ideas flashed in his mind.

He could sell it and make money. Stopping the truck, he turned off the engine and climbed down from the vehicle. He approached the bridge wall, stared at the object, and gasped. A corpse. He watched with wide eyes as a human body floated on the water. *Oh my God.*

He pulled out his phone and punched the numbers he knew by heart. Then he made the call.

***

Ray's body shimmered with heat as Loretta, who sat on top of him, glided her big ass up and down his stiff shaft. His fingers brushed her nipples, and he watched her face as she gasped. They were in his penthouse suite at the Sheraton Hotel. She had come to Lagos to open a new branch for her fashion house, which she recently named House of Loretta and had slept over for the night.

Ray held her tight and pumped into her in a steady rhythm, each sensation turning her body into a mass of needs and wants.

"Honey." She moaned and shut her eyes.

"Faster." Her voice was a command.

Ray had no choice but to obey. First, he pulled out as she frowned. Then, holding her tight, he flipped her onto the bed. Next, he drove his hard shaft into her until every inch was covered. Then, he thrust in and out, increasing his rhythm every second.

She called out his name, and he kept going. "I'm coming. Don't stop." Her voice was unsteady.

As Ray bent to kiss her, a smartphone rang. He looked up and saw it. It was his phone which he kept on the bedstand.

"Don't pick it!" Her voice had a tone of finality.

Ray nodded and continued to pump in and out of her wet heat.

"I'm so close. Keep going," she let out.

Ray held her wrist and caressed her skin as his shaft hit her G spot. She let out a sharp gasp.

The phone rang again. He pulled out, climbed out of bed, and picked up the gadget.

"No." Pain tinged Loretta's voice.

Ray held the phone to his ear and listened. "What? I'll be right there."

He dropped the phone and started dressing up, glancing at her.

Anger tightened her lips as she probed, "What is it about?"

"Honey, it's a case I'm working on. It's confidential."

"Is it about the final year university students who committed suicide? It's all over the news."

Ray stared at her for a long moment as he buttoned his white shirt. "Sweetheart, I'm not allowed to reveal any detail about the case to you. I'll call you."

He didn't wait for her to reply. Instead, he rushed to the door and stepped out of the room.

CHAPTER SIX

Ray climbed down the steps, walked through the hotel lobby, and out of the door. He got to his car, parked in the VIP sector, and hit the expressway three minutes later. The roads were busy even though it was early morning. On both sides of the road, pedestrians rushed to get to their destinations.

He frowned when he met traffic at Ebute Metta. He stayed in the traffic jam for ten minutes before the cars started moving again. He entered the Third Mainland Bridge twenty minutes later. He heaved a sigh of relief when he discovered no traffic on the bridge, considered the longest bridge in Nigeria.

Ray stopped when he reached where the rest of the team waited for him. He met Frank, Inspector James, Dr Kenneth, and three other police officers.

"Where is the body?" he asked, staring at Frank, and he followed his gaze to a corpse dripping with water close to a police cruiser.

"When did this happen?" he asked.

"He got a call from a truck driver at 4:15 am this morning. At first, he saw the body and thought it was a large fish, but when he stopped and observed closer, he discovered it was a human body floating on the lagoon. We got the confirmation about the location from him and came here forty minutes ago. Two members of our team pulled out the body with the help of three fishermen," James explained.

Ray stared at the corpse. It was the body of a young man he figured was in his late teens or early twenties. His eyes were wide, and his face carried a mark of torment and pain.

"What do we know about his identity?"

"His name is Peter Izigbemi. He is the son of Senator Pius Izigbemi, the Chief Whip of the Senate," James said.

Frank stepped closer and said, "Peter was a final year student at Lagos State University."

Another final year student, Ray thought as its implication left a bitter taste in his mouth.

He shifted his attention to the pathologist. "Doctor Kenneth, can you give us an estimated time of death?"

Dr Kenneth's face was tight. The strange death had sucked up everyone's energy. "Best guess is around 4 pm yesterday, an hour after he made his last Kedochat post," he said.

Ray's eyebrow shot up. "A Kedochat post?"

"Yes," James said. He withdrew a smartphone, opened the Kedochat app, and entered Peter's name on the search bar. The profile appeared. He clicked on it, scrolled, and stopped at a post with one thousand comments and sad face emojis.

James showed Ray the screen and read the written text. "Guys, I'm tired. I can't do this anymore."

Ray looked away sharply and stared at the hazy sky. Within the next minute, he lost all his energy as his body boiled with anger and sadness. He clenched his fist and took a deep breath. This had gotten far worse than they thought, and despite what the police claimed, no one had an idea of what was happening here.

CHAPTER SEVEN

"Where does Peter stay?" Ray asked James on the phone as he drove across the Third Mainland Bridge.

Frank sat beside him in the front seat.

"He lives in the University hotel. I just got information that the name of his friend is Isaiah Isoa. Both of them are roommates," James said.

James told him the hostel's name and the deceased's room number, and the call ended.

Ray put the GPS coordinates of the Lagos State University, known as LASU, in his car and drove faster. They reached the school an hour later after being stuck in the traffic.

Moremi hostel, where Peter lived, was an old building filled with male students. They passed two students who were washing clothes.

"Where can we locate Room 103?" Ray asked one of them.

"Climb the stairs and take a left. The numbers are written on top of the door. You will see the room."

Ray nodded and went inside the building. It was huge. A first-time visitor could easily get lost. Students poured in and out of the building. Ray knew most were rushing to their lectures. He heaved a sigh of relief when he saw the stairs.

He and Frank climbed the stairs and located room 103 three minutes later.

Frank knocked on the door. A wide-eyed boy in his early twenties opened it and stared at them. Tears filled his eyes as he sobbed.

"We are looking for Isaiah Isoa," Ray said, and both agents flashed their badges.

The boy wiped his tears and said, "That's me."

Ray nodded. "We want to ask you some questions about your friend, Peter. We know what happened. We are so sorry for your loss."

Isaiah's reply was covered with sobs. He moved aside and allowed them to enter the room.

The first thing Ray observed when they entered the room was that it was large. Four mattresses were placed neatly on the floor. Four gas cookers sat close to the right side of the wall. The room was neat, perhaps too neat for a boy's hostel room with four occupants.

Isaiah gave them two chairs, and they sat. He offered to get them a drink from the hostel cafeteria, but they declined.

Ray said, "What can you tell us about your friend, Peter? I checked the last Kedochat post he made. He said he couldn't take it anymore. What does he mean by that?"

"Peter suffered so much in his life. Things were never the same for him since his mother's death. Here, he always struggled to pay his school fees. I paid his last school fees. But I didn't know it was so bad that he had to make a Kedochat post and take his own life. I still can't believe he's gone." Isaiah choked up and started crying again.

Ray felt sad listening to Isaiah's words. Then, a thought entered his mind, and he arched his eyebrows. "Why did he have to suffer so much? His father is a senator."

"A respected member of the Senate," Frank added.

"Peter hated his father. They didn't communicate," Isaiah spat out the words and looked away.

Ray was filled with questions. "Why?"

Isaiah stared at them with angry eyes. "You don't know? Senator Pius is a wicked man. I blame him for Peter's death."

The harsh words made Ray narrow his eyes. This Isaiah was different from the young man who opened the door for them a few minutes ago. This was different from a picture he had built in his mind.

"I'm sorry. That came out wrong," Isaiah said.

Ray waved it off. "Don't worry about it. I get it. You have a right to be sad and angry. There are so many things going on that we don't know."

"Apart from his father, does Peter have any other close relative?" Frank asked.

"Peter had only one sibling—a sister who is married. She lives with her husband in Benin," Isaiah said.

Ray thanked Isaiah for his time and once again expressed his condolences.

As they left the building, Ray said to Frank, "This stinks. Tell our team to arrange transportation. I will be going to Benin. Stay here and speak with Peter's lecturers on Campus."

Frank nodded and left. Ray watched as Frank took a taxi to take him inside the campus.

Ray entered his car and drove off. As he passed the busy Lagos roads, he thought about Loretta. She must be pissed off at him by now. Their demanding jobs were adding a strain to their relationship. He pushed the thoughts to the back of his mind and focused on the case. He needed to get to Benin.

CHAPTER EIGHT

Ray arrived in Benin by noon via an Air Peace commercial flight. The Lagos State Police Command had arranged for him to be on the flight at the last minute. When the plane stopped at the runway of Benin Airport, passengers began to climb down.

Ray was dressed in a crisp white shirt and jeans. When he disembarked, the sun bathed his body with furious intensity.

Benin City was the capital of Edo State and the centre of the rubber industry in Nigeria. The city was linked by road to Sapele, Siluko, Okene and Ubiaja. Benin was the capital of the ancient kingdom of Benin, which flourished between the 13th and 19th centuries.

Ray entered a taxi and silently read the name of his destination.

"Where to?" the dark, burly driver with a beard asked.

"St Mark's Hospital."

The driver nodded and hit the road. The traffic in this modern city packed with high- and low-rise buildings and government offices was light, making the journey smooth. Within a few minutes, they reached the main square, passing the statue of

Emota, a woman honoured for assisting a 15th-century prince who later became Oba Ewuare.

They arrived at the hospital twenty minutes later. Ray paid the driver and alighted from the taxi.

St Mark's hospital was in an old one-storey building. Two cars were parked inside its gated and cemented compound. Ray showed the gatekeeper his badge, and the man directed him to the visitor's room, where he waited for Pete's sister, Stella Adiagbon.

Stella entered the room five minutes later. She wore thick glasses and looked more like a maths teacher than a nurse. Dark pimples covered her face. Ray showed her his badge and said, "Hi Stella, I am the one who called you on the phone. I'm Ray Okon, a DSS Agent working with the police on the case. I'm so sorry for your loss."

She looked away and used her white handkerchief to dab her teary eyes. She asked Ray questions about how the police found the body.

Ray provided her with the details and said, "Your late brother's friend, Isaiah, said he struggled to pay his school fees. Are you aware of this? When was the last time you saw him?"

Stella remained silent for a while. Ray couldn't read the expression behind the thick glasses.

"I saw him eight years ago when he came for my wedding," she said, appearing to be ashamed. "We are not too close, but he knows I care about him. Life has been tough for me and my family. My husband has been a mechanic since he lost his job three years ago. I provide for the family. Here—" she glanced across her surroundings, "—they haven't paid us for nine months. At weekends, I do extra jobs so my family can survive." Her voice was unsteady.

Ray frowned. "How can Peter be suffering when your father is a senator?"

Stella frowned when Ray mentioned her father. "Senator Pius is a heartless man. I don't want to talk about him." She turned to go, but Ray held her hand.

A wicked man. A heartless man. This was the second time someone described the senator that way.

Ray stared at her. "Please, Stella, I understand that you are angry. Tell us everything you know. It will help us in our investigation."

Stella considered his words and nodded.

"Isaiah said Peter hated his father. They didn't communicate. I observed you don't like him. Why? What caused the estrangement between father and son?" Ray asked.

"Our mother died of a heart attack after our father slept with her best friend. This made Peter hate our father," Stella said and paused. Her voice choked on a silent sob as she continued to speak. "My brother wouldn't have committed suicide. He was always strong. I can't still believe this. I put the blame on our father. He has finally gotten his wish. He is a wicked man and needs to be arrested," she said, using the handkerchief to wipe her tears.

Her voice was filled with emotions. What she said touched Ray, and he wondered what kind of father Senator Pius was. He tried to ask her more questions, but she excused herself and bolted out of the room.

Ray thought about what he heard and felt so sad for Peter. The family was a mess. As he stepped out of the hospital, he called James and discovered that Senator Izigbemi would be at his Benin residence the following day. He booked a hotel at Government Reserved Area (G.R.A) in the city and made plans to meet the senator the next day.

The puzzles, in this case, were rising like a storm. Ray was determined to get to the root of the University Students' Case.

CHAPTER NINE

Ray met Senator Pius at his residence in G.R.A after he finished a lunch meeting with five politicians in the State.

He arrived at the gated mansion and passed a statue at the centre of the compound with the inscription, Chief Linus Izigbemi (1930 - 2013). Two bikini-clad young ladies relaxed next to an Olympic-sized swimming pool. He walked across the compound and wondered why the senator was busy enjoying life while his son struggled to pay his fees at the university and eventually committed suicide.

When he entered the house, he waited in the living room while the senator was still in a meeting. The house had tiled walls, floors, and expensive paintings that hung on the walls. Ray noticed a large portrait of a woman in her early thirties. *Is she the senator's late wife?*

Everything in the house had a foreign feel, as though the items were all imported. The senator was a politician who would make big speeches about how best to develop the country but preferred to use imported products instead of encouraging local manufacturers. Wasn't that hypocrisy?

Sitting on the couch, he couldn't wait to see the man who had been described as *heartless* and *wicked*. But when the senator entered the living room an hour later, Ray was taken aback at seeing the man in front of him.

The senator was a little bit above average height. He was dark-skinned, lean, and soft-spoken. He had gentle and charismatic facial features that had everyone around him feel at ease. Wasn't that a unique trait that made politicians build a mass movement of people that helped them win elections?

He wore a long sleeve blue shirt and black trousers, unusual clothing for a Nigerian senator.

Ray had only seen him in pictures and on television. Senator Pius looked different in person.

As the senator approached him, Ray rose from the couch and said, "Sir, I'm DSS Agent Ray Okon. I'm sorry about what happened to your son. I'm consulting with the police on the case."

A sad smile appeared on the senator's face. "Welcome to my house, Ray. I hope I didn't delay you for long. I'm sorry."

They shook hands, and Ray noticed the senator's hands were soft as though he'd never worked hard.

"Not at all, sir."

The senator motioned for Ray to sit, and he sat opposite him. "What can I get for you? A drink perhaps."

Ray raised his hand. "Don't worry, sir."

"I insist. This is the first time you are coming to my house. Gbulie!" he called out.

A young man in his early twenties entered the living room, and the senator rattled orders. The boy returned a few minutes later with a bottle of red wine and two glasses. He filled the glasses and offered one to each of the men.

As they each took a sip, Ray began to ask the senator about his son. "I have spoken to your daughter and Peter's friend. I have read his last Kedochat post. We want to know exactly what went wrong."

The senator placed his glass on a red Formica table and stared at the wall opposite them while remaining quiet for a long moment. "I blame myself for what happened to Peter, to my family. It was my fault. I messed up." He dabbed a white handkerchief on his eyes. "I regret not mending the fence with my late son. Both of us were stubborn, but I should have made an effort to reach out to him. I failed him."

Ray remained quiet. He allowed the senator to calm down his emotions and mourn the loss of his son. He was staring at a father finally admitting his mistake, which was difficult for many men in the country.

When the senator finally looked at him, he said, "Thank you, Ray, for coming. I know what happened to my son, but I will give the police and DSS all the support they need." He put his fingers into his breast pocket and brought out a card. "Call me if you need anything." He handed the card to Ray.

Ray thanked him. Both men shook hands, and Ray left the building.

A nagging thought latched at the back of his mind on his way out of the compound. The senator had a sweet tongue, no doubt. He knew politicians were skilful liars and wondered whether the senator acted a script to make Ray believe him.

The senator's late son, Peter, struggled to pay his school fees while his father lived a life of luxury and had beautiful mansions and women across the country.

Did the senator have a hand in what happened to his son? Many things didn't make sense in this case. Nevertheless, Ray was determined to unravel the events to get to the truth.

CHAPTER TEN

After meeting with Senator Pius Izigbemi, Ray took a flight back to Lagos. When he reached Lagos, he received information from Frank that they would have an inter-agency meeting with the police at five in the evening. The time was 3 pm, and Ray used the next two hours to go through what he had discovered about the case, which wasn't much.

At 4:30 pm, he drove to Ikoyi, where the meeting would be held. He arrived by 4:50 and parked in front of a nondescript two-storey building owned by Lagos State Police Command, the venue for the meeting.

He met Frank at the entrance. They shook hands, and both entered the building. As they climbed the staircase, Ray shared what he had learnt from speaking with the victim's sister and father.

Frank said, "Peter's lecturer only had kind words to say about him. I met with a staff adviser who knew him personally. He said he didn't know Peter was going through a tough time. In his words, 'Peter always smiled and told me everything was fine.' I came back after staying there for three hours."

Ray took it all in and focused on the upcoming meeting. They reached the end of the staircase and entered a marbled corridor illuminated by bright lights.

"I heard some of our superiors would be here," Frank said when they reached the conference room door.

Ray pushed the door in, and both men entered.

Other DSS CID team members were already there—Dr Kenneth Akingbola, Sadiq Ibrahim, Chris Oluyemi, and Clement Emori. Chris Oluyemi and Clement Emori were their crime scene technicians. Sadiq Ibrahim was their photographer.

Top DSS analyst Christine Zainab, who came in afterwards, sat with two other DSS analysts at the other end of the table.

Inspector James Ibru and three police officers arrived minutes later. Gideon Owolabi, the head of DSS CID, was the last person to enter the conference room. He was tough-looking, a bull of a dark and six-foot-tall man, and well respected in the agency. Ray knew he studied Security at Oxford University and joined the agency twenty years ago. Gideon oversaw running the DSS Criminal Investigation Department in the country. He was efficient at his job and treated Ray with respect.

Ray had given him updates about the case while he was in Abuja. He got information from Frank that he arrived in Lagos today.

The conference room was large, with thick marbled floors and soundproof windows. A mahogany table surrounded by twenty-five chairs sat in the centre.

When everyone sat comfortably, Gideon said, "Where are we on the University Students' case?" He looked at Ray. "Ray, bring us up to speed."

Ray nodded and addressed the group for ten minutes. He took them through what he and his team had done since they started working on the case with the police. Then, he said, "We've interviewed friends and family of the victims. We are following all the leads, leaving no stone unturned. I just returned from Benin, where I met the sister and father of Peter Izigbemi. We are still trying to get the whole picture of what is going on before making deductions. The case is still ongoing. We are concerned about the strange deaths of the final-year students. We are working hard to get a clearer picture and ensure that such a terrible incident does not happen again."

Gideon tapped at his iPad's screen and looked up, focusing on James Ibru. "Let's hear from our colleague in the police force. James, go on."

James stood, fully dressed in his black police uniform. He said, "The police still maintains its position that these cases of suicide are fuelled by the pressure final year students in Nigerian universities face. From what we've gathered, the pressure is too much. Again, the evidence has also revealed underlying family and relationship problems which affected the victims and made them lose hope. We are working with the universities to ensure that the students are provided with competent counsellors to whom they should speak when facing depression or mental illness. The police work with facts. We have not yet seen contrary evidence that would make us change our initial position." He paused and looked around at the faces in the room. "However, with an open mind, we will continue to work with your agency to provide transparency, encourage the free flow of information and give you access to credible Intel."

Ray stared at him and thought James came prepared with a scripted speech. As the representative of the police, James was doing the bidding of his superiors. He hoped they were not playing politics with a case claiming lives. Ray pushed the thoughts out of his mind and focused on his boss, who spoke to James. "We want access to all the information you have on this case. What's happening in this case no longer looks good for our agencies. Nigerians want answers. We need to find them."

At that moment, the door opened, and a dark-skinned man said, "Here's what we've got so far in this case. Three suicide deaths. All of them are final year University students. Their last Kedochat posts have raised panic on social media. Their deaths had raised an uproar in the country." He looked around the room as the muscles in his face became distinct. "We still don't know why they took their own lives. We've got the government and politicians breathing down our neck to quickly solve this case, and we've got media attention of the worse kind. Unfortunately, our progress so far in this case is not enough." His voice vibrated in the room.

Ray didn't need anyone to remind him who this man was. Steve Maccido was the station chief of the DSS Lagos Branch.

Ray was surprised to see him. When he first arrived in Lagos, he reported to DSS Lagos Branch at Ikeja. They briefed him about the case and told him that James Ibru would be his point of contact in Lagos State Police Command. When he'd asked about the branch's station chief, they informed him Steve had travelled to South Africa on official duty and had been there for three months. Now, it was obvious he'd been following the case, and he looked angry.

Steve was plump and a little bit above average height. Like most of his superiors, Steve avoided long sermons and got to the point. Word had it that he saw inter-agency meetings as a waste of time and only wanted results from his subordinates.

"I want everyone to step up their efforts," Steve said. "Pursue all the leads. Unravel this case, find out what exactly is going on, and put an end to it."

He left the conference room without further discussion. The meeting ended three minutes later.

When Ray left the conference room and got to his office, he scribbled the names of the three victims on his notepad. He wrote a reminder to question the family of the first victim, Nonso Onyeama. Inspector James Ibru had told him the police had asked all his family members. Ray was determined to meet them. It was time to get to where it all started. That might help him get a new perspective on a case that sparked more questions than answers.

CHAPTER ELEVEN

Ray questioned Nonso Onyeama's mother about her son's death the next day. The family lived in a bungalow on Victoria Island, Lagos. When Ray met Nancy Onyeama, he saw that her clothes hung loosely on her body. Ray asked about Nonso's father, a senator representing Imo Central at the senate.

"My husband is not at home at the moment. He travelled to Abuja. Our son's death affected him deeply," she said.

For the next hour, Ray asked her questions about her son.

"Nonso is a good child. We raised him well. We provided for all his needs. He never got into trouble. He was always cheerful and happy. We are close. I'm still shocked that he had to take his own life," she said, eyes vacant, staring at the wall.

Ray used the next two hours to question the late boy's brothers and sisters. They answered all his questions and cried as they talked about Nonso. None of them knew what went wrong. The family was kind to Ray and invited him to join them for lunch. He did.

They ate pounded yam, and vegetable soup garnished with fish.

He consoled them, dropped his card, and promised to stay in touch.

When he returned to his hotel room in the evening, he was exhausted and needed to rest. So, he undressed and bathed. When he came out of the bathroom, a thought flashed in his mind. *Loretta.*

Ray looked at the corner of his room where she kept her bag. His eyebrow shot up when he discovered it was no longer there.

He called her number and received an outgoing message. "You have reached Loretta Olawale. Please, leave a message," a female voice said.

Ray pressed another number. It rang twice before the person at the other end picked up.

"Where is your madam?" he asked Jane, Loretta's secretary.

"She is back here in Abuja," Jane said at the other end of the line.

Confusion filled Ray. She didn't tell him. Was it because of their little quarrel? He'd been occupied by the job and was hoping to apologize when he returned today. Now, she was gone.

"Where is she now? Is she in the office?"

"No, she is in a meeting."

"Tell her to call me when she is through with the meeting."

***

Garki, Abuja
"Madam, he called you when you were in the meeting," Jane said when Loretta entered the adjoining room that led to her office.

Loretta was dressed in a blue pinstripe suit and high heels. She was glad the meeting was successful. She had just closed a deal with a wealthy client to supply designer women's evening wear to their stores.

She narrowed her eyes and stared at her secretary. "Who?"

"Ray Okon," Jane said.

Fury built within Loretta. *He finally has time for us*, she thought. "What did he say?"

"He said I should tell you to call him when you are through with the meeting."

Loretta's anger spiked, and she walked into her office. *How dare he?*

Since he led her on and left her hung and dry, she hadn't heard from him. He'd left the room and refused to tell her about his work even when she told him hers and had walked out like she didn't exist. Now, he had remembered her and had started calling.

True, their jobs were stressing their relationship, but Ray—the love of her life—was too rigid and principled, and it had started getting on her nerves.

She didn't want to think about this. She didn't want anything that would spoil her mood. She went to sit on her chair. Then she pushed the thoughts out of her mind, opened her laptop, and started going through her unread email messages.

CHAPTER TWELVE

Daran Hassan sat at his desk reading an Engineering textbook in Kashim Ibrahim Library at Ahmadu Bello University but couldn't concentrate. Since he came back from morning lectures, he had been in the library for the past two hours surrounded by other students who sat behind their desks and laptops, studying for their examinations which would begin in three weeks.

The library building was huge with thick pillars, large columns, and walls. The university sat at the centre of Zaria in Kaduna State, in the northern part of the country.

It was ten on Friday morning. The cloud outside darkened, threatening rain while mirroring the conflicting thoughts on Daran's mind. He was worried about his best friend, Destiny Magu. Both were final-year students at the university where they studied Civil Engineering.

Until two months ago, Destiny used to be cheerful and vibrant. The students adored him. Why wouldn't they? Destiny was the president of the Student Union Government (SUG). His father, Senator Vincent Magu, was the chairman of the Armed Services Committee in the Senate and a respected man. Destiny's mother worked as a news broadcaster in Kaduna. That was not all. Destiny's girlfriend was the popular Tricia Bello, one of the most beautiful girls on campus.

Destiny had it all. His future was set. He lived the Nigerian dream. And yet, Destiny didn't allow his family wealth to make him look down on others. Despite his flashy cars and enormous family fortune, he brought himself down to the level of his fellow students. Daran liked his friend because he was kind and walked the talk. When he campaigned for the position of President of SUG, he promised to change the rotten system and implement bold ideas to improve the students' lives. Today, the students called Destiny their hero.

Destiny's SUG government changed the old system. They partnered with the school's Work Department to refurbish the hostels and led a campaign that made the school authorities cancel their plan to increase the school fees. They even struck a rare deal with Taxi Drivers Association in ABU to reduce the price of school taxis by fifty percent. That was his friend, Destiny. He had been a blessing in his life. But everything changed two months ago when Destiny became withdrawn and broke up with his heartthrob, Tricia. Then, he stopped attending lectures. When Daran started calling him to find out why Destiny stopped picking up his calls.

Other students noticed it and became concerned. He was their SUG President. They needed to know what was going on. They reached out to Daran because he was the only student closest to the Student Union President. Daran was lost for words at what was going on and how fast his great friendship with Destiny went downhill without notice. He didn't have a clue about what was going on. He, too, wanted answers, and the situation deeply troubled him.

Daran tried to study again, but it was a futile effort. His mind was not at rest. Finally, he snapped his textbook shut and sat ramrod straight. He shut down his laptop and put it in his bag.

He stood and walked close to the window. The clouds were dark, and it had started drizzling. Some students began to leave the library, perhaps to return to their lodges and remove the washed clothes they spread outside their rooms for the sun to dry.

Daran returned to his seat and brought out his phone. He'd left Destiny several messages on his Kedochat messenger, but Destiny hadn't replied. Worse, Daran had not seen nor heard from Destiny for the past four weeks.

He opened his Kedochat app, received a new notification, and his eyes narrowed. Someone had mentioned him in the comments section of a post. He clicked the alert, which took him to the message. The online announcement had five thousand comments and sad face emojis. His eyes widened when he saw that Destiny had made the post an hour ago.

He read the post. "Finally, I will be free and get the peace I deserve."

What the hell? No, Destiny! Daran packed his bag with speed as his heart raced and his hands trembled.

When he was done, he rose, took his bag, and sprinted across the long length of the library hall, hitting someone by the shoulder. "Sorry," he muttered and climbed down the stairs.

Daran stepped out of the building, and the drizzle hit him in the face, but it couldn't deter him. He stopped a school taxi.

"Where to?" the young driver at the steering asked.

"The school's main gate."

He entered the taxi and paid the driver. The vehicle winded through tarred roads, passing faculty buildings and a beautiful mosque. Daran rushed out like a mad man when they reached the school gate.

"Your bag," the driver shouted.

"Oh," Daran said, ran back and picked it.

He entered another taxi that took him to 10 Jamaa Road, where Destiny lived off-campus. Destiny lived in a two-bedroom flat in a beautiful residential two-storey building.

As Daran entered the well-kept compound and climbed the stairs, he brought out a spare key Destiny had given him. He hoped Destiny had not changed the lock.

When he reached the room, he slid the key inside the keyhole and turned it. Luckily for him, it worked. His trembling hands turned the handle and opened the door. He entered the living room, and a foul smell slammed hard against his nostrils. Daran turned on the light, and the scene that met him weakened his legs. He let out a gasp and began to shout.

CHAPTER THIRTEEN

The putrid smell hit Ray's nose as he and Frank entered the room. Other members of their team, Dr Kenneth, Sadiq Ibrahim, Chris Oluyemi, and Clement Emori, joined them two minutes later.

Ray glanced across the room and saw Inspector James Ibru conversing quietly with two uniformed police officers. Their eyes met, and they greeted silently.

The living room of the two-bedroom flat was large. An LG 40-inch flat-screen television hung at the centre of the wall. A woofer sound system sat under the TV. Two sofas were placed on opposite sides. A MacBook Pro Laptop and two smartphones sat on top of a stool to the right. Photographs of Destiny with his family and friends hung on the wall. Ray's eyes rested on the childhood picture of Destiny. His parents surrounded him, their faces bright with smiles. Destiny appeared to be ten in the photo. He looked innocent, so young and full of life, unaware of the evil in the world.

Ray shifted his gaze from the picture and stared at the body in the centre of the room. A steel chair sat close to it. The DSS CID photographer— Sadiq Ibrahim, a dark, lanky man in his mid-forties, snapped pictures of the body and the two rooms.

When he finished, Ray stepped closer to the body. Everyone in the room was quiet, sadness clouding their faces. They all wore gloves so that they would not contaminate the room.

Ray and his team members had flown from Lagos to Kaduna when they heard the terrible news. They had arrived in the afternoon. James and his fellow police officers had gotten there thirty minutes earlier.

Frank joined him and said, "This is different from the pattern we've seen in this case. He didn't jump into the lagoon but died in his room. The death is suspicious and doesn't look like suicide. It—"

"It sure does," Inspector James cut in. He moved to the right corner of the room and picked up an object that looked like a bottle. As he showed the bottle to Ray and Frank, others approached them to see the item.

Ray studied the bottle. It had the name 'Sniper' across it.

"This is Sniper, a pesticide that is designed to kill rats. But it kills human beings too," James explained. He glanced at Dr Kenneth. "Am I correct, doctor?"

"Yes," Dr Kenneth said. "It's a highly poisonous substance."

"Doctor, can you tell us the time of death and give us an idea of how he died?" James said.

"I can only make a guess," Dr Kenneth said as he stared at the corpse. "The time of death is between 8 to 11 am on Friday morning."

"The doctor is correct. He made a Kedochat post by 8 am yesterday morning and probably killed himself a few minutes after that," a police officer who stood beside James said. He held a smartphone in his hand.

They stared at him, and he showed them Destiny Magu's Kedochat profile. Ray read the post, which had over ten thousand comments. "Finally, I'll be free and get the peace I deserve."

Someone in the group let out a gasp. Ray looked away, his eyes filled with tears.

"I guess he took the Sniper drink in his room and collapsed on the floor when he reached the living room," Dr Kenneth said.

Ray wiped his tears and looked back at the corpse, visualizing how he died. He said, "It doesn't explain why the chair is close to his body. I think he took Sniper while sitting on the chair and went down on the floor when he began to feel the effects of the drink. He probably died on the floor a few minutes after taking the poisonous drink."

"We will find out more about what happened here when we do the autopsy," Dr Kenneth said.

James ordered the crime scene techs—Chris Oluyemi and Clement Emori—and two police officers to carry the corpse and load it into the police van now parked in the compound.

Ray watched as the men covered the body in a white bedsheet, laid it on a stretcher, and carried it out of the room. The corpse would be taken to Kaduna State Police Command. Then Dr Kenneth would work with other technicians from the police force to do the autopsy and write his official report.

The smell of death in the room made Ray feel sick. The boy's death was strange. As Frank observed, despite what the police believed, this was different from the pattern. The deaths were spreading across Nigerian Universities like wildfire.

A dangerous pattern had developed in this case. Ray was sure of that. He didn't want to think of its frightening implication. It was no longer a coincidence that those final-year students took their own lives. Right now, the evidence made it look that way.

When Ray stepped out of the building, the cold October air blasted his face. He clenched his fist, his determination firm. Nothing would stop him until he had unravelled what was going on here.

CHAPTER FOURTEEN

Hundreds of students filled the open field at Ahmadu Bello University. They wore black clothes. Some of the girls wore hijabs. Others wore a headscarf. The students carried placards, lighted candles, and sang 'Solidarity is forever.'

It was seven on Wednesday evening. Ray and Frank had stayed in Zaria, Kaduna, for four days to attend the candlelight vigil the university students held in honour of their late SUG President, Destiny Magu. His death had thrown the whole country into a frenzy. The media talked about him in their TV programs, showing pictures and videos of the late student leader. Throughout that day, #RIPDestinymagu trended on social media.

Ray watched the students as they cried and mourned his loss. Some carried placards that read, "Till we meet again, Destiny." While others displayed, "Rest in peace, Destiny."

A group of students wore white polos with pictures of Destiny Magu.

"I guess they are his classmates," Frank said beside him.

"Greatest Nigerian students!" a voice in a microphone bellowed and began to address the students. "We are here to pay our final respect to our great leader, Destiny Magu, who...."

Ray and Frank moved to a less crowded location.

As they walked, someone behind them shouted, "He didn't have to die. He was the only child of his parents."

Frank looked around the field and said, "The students adore him."

"It's obvious," Ray said.

A young girl carrying a small placard that displayed 'RIP great leader' cried as she walked past them.

A wave of emotions hit Ray like a tornado, and he felt terrible for the senseless death of the young student leader.

Ten minutes later, members of SUG executives who stood at the podium invited students to give testimonies about their encounter with Destiny. Ray and Frank watched with renewed interest.

A dark slim boy climbed to the podium. A female SUG executive who stood beside him gave him the microphone. "My name is Lawrence. I'm a third-year student. After I lost my parents in an accident, I had no one to pay my school fees. When I told Destiny about it, he told me not to worry, that he would take care of it. It's hard to believe he's gone."

When the boy left, the female SUG executive collected the microphone and said, "My name is Jennifer. I'm a member of the SUG executive. Destiny's death hit us like a whirlwind. No one saw it coming. Destiny took us like his family. He would always tell us to address him by his first name. He encouraged us to bring fresh ideas to the team. He was so kind and gentle. Rest in peace, Destiny. You left us too soon."

The testimonies continued, and Ray prepared to leave. Someone touched his shoulder. He looked back at Frank, who pointed to the person at the podium. A short, plump young man in his mid-twenties was finishing his speech. "Destiny, you ensured I became a better man. Thank you for your great friendship. I weep when I remember all the plans we made and all the goals you wanted to achieve," he choked and broke down in tears. "It's too early for you to leave. Please, come back."

"Who is that?" Ray asked.

"Let me find out," Frank said and left.

He returned five minutes later. "His name is Daran Hassan. He is Destiny's best friend," he said.

"He would probably be the man who knew Destiny more than anyone else," Ray said to Frank. "Set up a meeting with Daran. Let's meet him tomorrow."

Frank nodded, and they left the field.

* * *

That night at Ray's four-star hotel room in Graceland, a small neighbourhood in Zaria, he was worried as he thought about Destiny's death. He needed to get a clearer picture of who Destiny was.

He went to the bathroom and rinsed his face. Then, he brought out his smartphone and opened the Kedochat app when he returned to the bedroom.

Ray searched for Destiny Magu's Kedochat profile and got it. He clicked it open and started scrolling. He saw the last post Destiny made. "Finally, I'll be free and get the peace I deserve." The post now had 14000 comments. Destiny had posted it last Friday morning. Ray had seen it twice.

He clicked the comments section and read some of the comments.

"No, Destiny!"

"Rest in peace, Destiny."

"Destiny, what are you saying?"

A teardrop gathered in Ray's right eye. He scrolled down to see the next post. It showed a picture of Destiny with three young men and three women. The person who sat in the middle was a woman in her mid-fifties. They wore bright smiles on their faces. The post read:

With other executives of the National Association of Nigerian Students (NANS), and the Minister of Education, Amina Rafique, after she finished delivering a keynote address at today's convocation ceremony. She promised that her ministry would work with National University Commission to provide for the welfare of the students in Nigerian Tertiary Institutions.

Ray scrolled to the next post. The picture showed two men—an older man and a young man Ray observed was Destiny. They wore black suits and stood outside an office. Destiny wrote, "I just finished a meeting with our vice-chancellor. He is happy with the performance of our SUG leadership and promised to give us the support we need."

The following post caught Ray's attention. It had 20,000 comments and many heart emojis. It showed Destiny in a group photograph with three dark-skinned middle-aged men. Ray read the post:

Today is a great day in the history of student unionism in our great citadel of learning. After weeks of campaigns, protests, and meetings, my SUG team and I have finally done it. I just finished a meeting with the chairman of the ABU Taxi Drivers' Association. We reached an agreement to reduce the price of taxis on Campus by 50 percent.

Ray clicked the comments section and saw comments from students who hailed Destiny as their hero. The rest of Destiny's posts on his Kedochat profile covered his achievements during his tenure as the Student Union President.

It was evident to Ray that Destiny's Kedochat profile was a powerful curriculum vitae of a young, vibrant student leader who cared for the welfare of the students. At such a young age, he already had an excellent record and was on the path to greatness. Ray had gotten the information that his father was a senator. It was also clear that he followed in his father's footsteps and would have succeeded in politics. *If he had lived,* Ray thought.

From his investigation, Ray discovered that his family had enormous wealth. Destiny had flashy cars and lived in a two-bedroom flat. He was a friend of lecturers, and the school authorities held him in high regard. Despite the hardship in the country, Destiny lived the Nigerian dream and was likeable and adored by the students.

All that begged the obvious question, why did Destiny take his own life? He had so much to live for. Was his death somehow connected to the other final-year students suspected of taking their own lives? Ray was determined to find out.

CHAPTER FIFTEEN

Early Thursday afternoon, Ray parked the cruiser Kaduna police gave him in front of Ali Akilu hostel. He was with his team member, Frank. When he cut the engine, they climbed out of the car.

The male hostel where Daran lived was an old three-storey building with massive pillars and railings. Each floor had a long open corridor. Ray figured the male students left their clothes outside their rooms to dry under the sun.

Daran lived on the ground floor. They walked to room number twenty, knocked, and heard approaching footsteps. The door opened, a face appeared, and Ray recognized the bulky young man with a short frame who said kind words and mourned his friend the day before at the candlelight vigil.

He wore a T-shirt, blue jeans, and brown sandals. Glasses perched on his nose, and he carried a laptop bag on his shoulder and a textbook in his hands.

He placed one palm on the doorjamb, his eyes filled with concern. "Who are you?"

Ray flashed his badge. "I'm Ray Okon. My partner is Frank Igwe. We are DSS agents."

"I didn't do anything wrong," Daran said, his eyes alert.

Frank walked closer to him and said, "We know you didn't do anything wrong. We just want to ask you some questions about your late friend, Destiny Magu."

Daran lifted his right hand and checked his watch. "I don't have the time. I have an exam on Tuesday. I'm rushing to go and study. I'm already late."

"Where to?"

"Library."

Ray knew his type—always anxious during the examination periods and afraid they would fail if they didn't study enough.

Ray touched his shoulder and looked straight into his eyes. When he held his gaze, he said, "This won't take more than five minutes. I promise."

"Alright, make it quick," Daran said.

He stepped aside and allowed them to enter the room.

The room was large, spartan, but well arranged. Four mattresses lay on the floor. The table at the centre of the room was filled with books and photocopied documents. Pictures of Daran and his best friend hung on the wall.

Ray and Frank sat on two plastic chairs. Daran sat beside them on a worn-out metal chair, his feet tapping on the floor.

Ray held Daran's gaze and said, "When I heard you speak during yesterday's candlelight vigil, I knew you'd lost your closest friend. We are working with the police to find out why Destiny took his own life. We are so sorry for your loss."

"Thank you," Daran said, his voice low, his face contemplative.

"You and Destiny were very close," Frank said. "We would like to know more about his personality."

"Destiny was the happiest guy I knew. He was easy-going, energetic, and generous," Daran started. "He cared deeply about the student's welfare and changed the rotten system that made students suffer for years in this school. He had been voted the best SUG President in the history of this university by the school Alma Mater Association. Destiny was my best friend. He shared his dreams and goals with me. Right now, as I talk about him, it is as if I'm dreaming. It's difficult to accept that he's gone."

"Please, give us a timeline of what happened when you noticed changes in his behaviour," Ray said.

"Destiny had always been lively and a bundle of energy," Daran said. "The students loved him. He lit up every room he entered. Everything changed two months ago when he told me he was ready to engage his girlfriend."

"What's her name?" Frank asked.

"Tricia Bello."

Ray scribbled on his notepad and said, "Go on."

"They love each other so much," Daran continued. "Tricia was beautiful and smart. She was Miss Pharmacy in her faculty. They were known as the super couple on campus. It made sense. Destiny had what it took to take care of her. He was an only child and the heir to his family wealth. Tricia's father is a professor at this university. Her mother works as an accountant at First Bank of Nigeria. Their future was set. Destiny showed me the diamond ring he planned to use for the engagement, and I told him to go ahead." He paused and used a handkerchief to dab at his eyes, which were beginning to water.

Ray and Frank gazed at him, listening to every word he said.

"I was so happy for him," Daran continued. "One week later, he told me he'd broken up with her."

"Did you find out why?" Frank asked, his face tight.

"Yes, I asked him why. He said he didn't want to talk about it. Next, he stopped coming to lectures. Then, he stopped talking to me and anyone else. He preferred to keep to himself and got angry at any slightest thing. I was shocked. The Destiny I knew vanished. I became worried and didn't understand what was happening. It got worse. Destiny became distant, and our great friendship suffered along with it.

"We stopped talking, and I gave him his space. Six weeks later, I became worried because I no longer saw him in school. The day it happened, I came to his room and discovered that he had killed himself." Tears filled Daran's eyes. He stopped talking and sobbed uncontrollably.

Ray held his hand and consoled him. Moments later, he brought out his handkerchief again and wiped the tears on his face.

Ray and Frank exchanged glances. They had listened to everything he said with rapt attention. Rising from the chair, Ray dropped his card on the table.

"We will keep in touch, Daran. Please, contact me if there is anything else you remember. We are investigating a case of suicide deaths involving final-year students from different universities in our country. The deaths are strange. Destiny's death is similar to the ones we are investigating. Your information may help us understand what is happening and stop more students from dying."

Daran nodded, a frown appearing on his face.

Ray walked towards the door but paused as a thought occurred to him. "Do you have Tricia Bello's phone number? We'd like to speak to her."

Daran nodded, brought out his phone, and called out her digits. Ray saved the details on his smartphone and thanked him.

Both agents left the hostel and got into their vehicle five minutes later.

Frank was the first to speak. "The whole thing about Destiny's death is weird."

"Yes, it is," Ray said as his hands tightened on the steering.

This was supposed to be an open and shut case. But now, the puzzles and unanswered questions had tripled.

CHAPTER SIXTEEN

That evening, Ray and Frank got to Tricia Bello's neighbourhood. She lived in a one-bedroom apartment in a student's lodge, five kilometres from the University campus.

When they knocked on her door, a slim light-skinned girl opened it slightly and popped out her head. Ray showed his badge and explained who they were.

"I'm sorry Tricia is not here, but I can tell you where she is. I'm her friend, Angela. I hope there is no problem."

"None at all, Angela," Frank said.

"Tricia left here yesterday and hasn't come back since then. Right now, she is at the lecturers' quarters where her family lives."

"Where is that?" Ray asked.

She gave them directions back to the main campus. They thanked her and left. Ray drove back inside the school, passing Dogon Yaro trees along a well-paved road.

The time was six in the evening, and streetlights illuminated the roads on the campus. He followed the direction Angela had given him, passed a bend after a church building, and drove straight to the lecturers' quarters.

The residential neighbourhood was quiet. Beautiful gardens in front of cabin-like houses. When he reached a home marked 505, he slowed down and entered the small compound. Ray parked the car in front of the cabin, cut the engine, and the men alighted.

They walked to the front door, and Frank pressed the bell. When it rang, they heard approaching footsteps.

A dark-skinned young lady in a blue gown opened the door and glared at them. "What do you want?"

Ray flashed his badge. "I'm Ray Okon. We are DSS Agents. We are working with the police on an investigation. We would like to talk to Tricia Bello. Her friend told us she lives here."

The girl stepped out and, like a sentinel, rested her back against the door frame. "Why do you want to see her?"

"We need her help," Frank said. "We'll like to ask her a few questions about Destiny Magu."

The girl's jaw tightened the moment she heard the name. But, when she spoke, her voice softened. "I'm sorry. Tricia is here, but she doesn't want to see anyone. We don't know what happened to her. Our family doctor will come and check on her tomorrow to know what happened to her. She's been numb, her eyes vacant since Destiny died."

"Are you her sister?" Frank asked.

"Yes, I'm her younger sister," she said.

"What is your name?" Ray asked.

"My name is Sandra."

"Alright, Sandra. We know your family is seeking answers. We want to help too. We know Destiny and Tricia were engaged shortly before he died. What can you tell us about their relationship?" Ray asked.

"Destiny called off the engagement and killed himself a few weeks later. That's what happened," Sandra snapped, her voice laced with anger.

Ray figured she was angry at the late SUG President for breaking her sister's heart.

"Right now, my sister is devastated because of what happened to Destiny," Sandra said.

"But he loved her, right?" Frank asked.

"Yes. They were so in love with each other. They had been together since their second year at the university. It was as if they were created for each other. Everyone around them knew the next thing was marriage. When Destiny engaged my sister and broke up with her a week later, I thought he'd gone insane."

"Was there anything she did that made Destiny call off their engagement?"

Sandra shook her head. "None. My sister cried for days. She said she didn't do anything wrong. The whole thing was strange. We don't know what happened to Destiny. I hope this doesn't destroy my sister's life."

Ray gave her his card. "Thank you, Sandra. If you remember anything else, no matter how insignificant you think it is, don't hesitate to call me."

She collected the card and nodded.

Ray and Frank left afterwards.

CHAPTER SEVENTEEN

Ray and Frank left Zaria Friday morning and travelled to Kaduna, the state capital. They arrived an hour later. Ray had already called Senator Magu and set up a meeting at his residence for 11 am.

Senator Vincent Magu lived in the Government Reserved Area known as GRA. It was a place for wealthy businesspeople and top government officials. The senator was both. DSS CID analysts had gotten information that the senator was from Benue, a state in the middle belt region of the country, but he established businesses in Kaduna. The senator dealt in many things, including cement manufacturing and a chain of Magu retail stores spread across the country. However, most of his money came from his oil company, where he raked in billions of Naira.

Ray drove through Ali Akilu Road and headed into the Kaduna city centre. Finally, he reached Joseph Abbi Street in G.R.A, a quiet neighbourhood where the senator lived. He stopped when he arrived in front of a giant metal gate surrounded by high walls covered in white paint. A uniformed security man carrying a metal detector approached them.

"Do you have an appointment with Senator Magu?"

Ray told him yes. The security man placed a quick phone call and confirmed the identity of the two visitors.

He ran the metal detector around the car. Then, he opened the gate a minute later, and Ray drove in and parked the car inside the compound.

Both agents alighted from the car, and Ray took time to observe the unfamiliar environment.

The residence was large and adorned with flowers and beautiful trees. Ray counted nine parked cars. More cars streamed through the gate after the security man confirmed their identity. Ray figured those were VIPs who came to console the senator on losing his son.

The three-storey building at the centre of the compound was painted white. Ray spotted a DSTV satellite dish mounted on the aluminium roof.

Ray and Frank climbed the stone steps leading to a half-open glass door. They entered a large room where the senator was entertaining visitors. The room was filled with comfortable chairs set up in distinct sections.

Ray spotted Magu, surrounded by three politicians. The senator was a big bull of a man in a flamboyant blue *Agbada* and shook hands with his visitors. When he saw Ray and his partner, he said to the people around him, "Excuse me, please."

He motioned for Ray and Frank to follow him.

They followed him as he entered a long corridor decorated with a Persian rug. They climbed a long winding staircase that stopped in front of another hallway. The senator took a right, opened the door to a room by his left, and ushered them in. Ray knew the room was his private study.

A long bookcase ran along the length of the well-furnished twelve-by-twelve room.

The senator lowered his body into the chair behind the desk. "Please, sit. Make yourself comfortable. Welcome. I'm glad you are working on this case."

"Thank you, sir. We will get to the root of this case," Ray said.

Senator Magu offered them a drink. They declined.

"We are sorry for your loss, sir," Frank said. "It's painful when a father loses his child."

"Destiny was my only son. He was also my only child. I never believed this would happen. He wanted to follow in my footsteps and go into politics after graduation, but he was so stubborn. If he had listened to me, he would still be alive today."

"You said 'if he had listened to you.' What happened?" Ray asked.

"Destiny got admission to study at Harvard University in the United States, but he rejected it and opted to study at ABU, Zaria."

Ray narrowed his eyes. "Why?"

"His patriotism had always been there since he was young, but sometimes, it made him too idealistic. He told me, 'Dad, if I leave, who will stay?'"

Ray and Frank exchanged glances. Ray admired Destiny's courage in knowing what he'd wanted and going for it.

"We had a heated argument about it. Finally, his mum intervened and told me to allow him to do what he wanted. Today, that decision to allow him to not study abroad has cost him his life. That's my biggest regret in life," the older man said, wiping his chubby face with a white handkerchief.

"Sir, do you have an idea of what happened to your son or why he took his own life?" Frank asked.

"No. I have no idea," the senator said. His eyes were empty as he stared absentmindedly at the wall.

"Sir." Ray's voice brought him back out of his reverie.

Senator Magu's phone rang. He picked up the call and listened. When he was done, he rose and walked around his desk to where Ray and Frank sat. Both men stood as he approached them.

He shook their hands firmly. "Thank you for coming. Please, help me find out what happened to my son."

He gave Ray his card to contact him via his mobile number if they needed anything.

The bright sunshine blinded them when they stepped out of the door. As Ray walked to the car, the image of the senator begging him to help him find what happened to his late son filled his mind. He and his team needed answers fast. Unfortunately, the more they searched for answers, the more they returned to square one. This case had become a hard nut to crack, and the clock was ticking.

CHAPTER EIGHTEEN

Ray and Frank took a flight back to Lagos after meeting Senator Magu. They reached Lagos in the afternoon and joined other team members in an impromptu inter-agency briefing at Ikeja, featuring members of the police and DSS.

Steve Maccido, Gideon Owolabi, James Ibru, and Lagos State Deputy Commissioner of Police Dennis Depriye sat in the conference room, their facial expressions ranging from sad to furious. Junior officers and agents working on the case were also present.

Dennis rose and dropped a vanguard newspaper on the table. "The media has ripped us apart, claiming that we've not put in enough effort to solve the case. They blamed everyone involved in the investigation. If you can't get your act right, heads will roll. We can't tolerate this. This has made both our agencies look bad. In the mind of the public, we are incompetent. We will take you all off the case if you don't start getting results."

The rest of their superiors made similar statements. The meeting was brief and ended after fifteen minutes.

When Ray entered his hotel room late in the evening, he was exhausted. He undressed, took his bath, and collapsed on the bed.

He woke up in the middle of the night, panting. Images of the dead students tortured his mind and gave him nightmares. When he opened his eyes, beads of sweat sprang to his face. The exhaustion he felt kept him awake. The demanding work and toil he'd put in this case were beginning to take their toll on him. He knew his body was stressed because they were not making headway. Worse, his superiors had threatened to take them off the case if they didn't make progress.

He wiped the sweat clinging to his forehead and reached for the other side of the bed with his hand. It was empty. Thoughts of Loretta crept into his mind. He needed her now more than ever. He missed her. He knew she hated his guts right now because she was angry at him.

Their jobs had always been demanding. However, they had managed to strike the right balance. But this case had put a wedge between them.

Ray turned on his bed and sighed. Nothing was working in both his professional and personal life. An image of Loretta's warm smile crept into his mind. He needed her by his side and missed her touch, but he knew what to do.

***

Garki, Abuja
Loretta sat at her desk, perusing a glossy fashion magazine. She was stylishly dressed in a pink figure-

hugging sleeveless gown that moulded to her hips and thighs. Her long dark hair was secured atop her head in a ponytail. She made sure she looked her best with a final glance in the mirror that morning.

She smiled when she noticed that the magazine featured one of her designs in this month's edition. It was a special women's evening wear from her newest collection, which she'd designed. She looked around the office and relaxed in her recliner.

Business was good, and House of Loretta had just established its first branch in Lagos. She had started making plans to expand to other states. She hoped it would be a massive success.

Loretta loved her work. She started tailoring right from her university days. She had distinguished role models, but her late mother, Campbell Olawale, a skilful tailor, was her inspiration. Immediately after she graduated from the University of Lagos, she took advanced courses in fashion design, did an internship in the famous House of Lara, and launched her business. The journey had been challenging but fruitful. Sometimes, she wished her mother was alive to see her baby girl living her dreams.

She heard a slight noise and looked up. The door opened, and Jane entered carrying a file. She set it on her table and said, "Go through it one last time, ma'am. It contains the vision of House of Loretta and important key points you need to make the best pitch to the investors during tomorrow's meeting."

Loretta collected the file and began to peruse it.

"You need to be on your best, ma'am. This meeting could get us the funds we need for the expansion," Jane said.

Loretta smiled, glad the woman was on her team. "Thank you, Jane. I appreciate all the efforts you are putting into this."

Jane had proven her competence in the workplace. She was not just a secretary but her cheerleader and confidante.

Jane smiled and left the office. Loretta studied the document for the next two hours and worked on getting her pitch ready. When she was done, she started typing a letter on her PC.

A few minutes later, she heard the door open and frowned. "Not now, Jane. I don't need disturbance."

She resumed work, but the familiar scent of cologne hit her nose. *What is that?*

Loretta furrowed her brow and looked up. Ray stood in her office holding a flower vase of cute red roses. He looked impeccably dressed in blue chinos and a striped, white T-shirt that hung perfectly on his body. His outfit complemented his dark complexion. He was clean-shaven, and his short hair looked good on his athletic body.

She noticed his compact abdominal muscles. *Had he been working out in the gym?* She should be angry at him. Why was she excited that he came bearing gifts?

Ray's five-foot-ten shadow approached her desk. He placed the flower in front of her. "I'm so sorry, honey. I was foolish."

Her anger faded, and tears filled her eyes. He leaned over the desk and took her hand. She allowed him to kiss her hand.

She rose. They rounded the desk and hugged each other tightly. *Oh, God.* She'd missed him, his gentle touch, and his voice.

Ray lifted her face and caressed her neck with soft kisses as the thoughts swirled in her mind. Heat suffused her skin, and she took a sharp breath.

When he placed his lips on hers, it was too good to resist. She curled her body on his and enjoyed his soft, teasing kisses, a promise of something more. Then, the kiss became intense, and Loretta dropped the file in her hand.

Ray disengaged his lips from hers, and she frowned.

"A second, please." He brought out his phone and switched it off. "Sweetheart, I want to taste every inch of you. The rest of the world can go to hell."

Her heart raced, and her breath became erratic. Heat and anticipation pulled between her legs. He took her hand, and they walked out of the office.

"Jane, cancel my appointments for the day," Loretta said on their way out of the office.

CHAPTER NINETEEN

Ray drove Loretta to his new apartment. It was evening, and time was edging closer to six. He'd moved into a bigger apartment at Maitama, a well-furnished three-bedroom bungalow, two months ago. He'd converted one of the rooms to his study where he worked when he came home. He liked the neighbourhood. It was quiet and well secured. His new promotion at the agency and a higher pay-check helped him afford the high-end home.

When he reached his place, his gateman saw him and opened the gate. Then, he drove the car into the compound and parked in front of his house.

They left the car, and Loretta waited while he punched the numbers in the security panel close to the door. After he'd switched off the alarm, he opened the door. He gazed at her longingly; their need for each other flooded their eyes. He placed his hand on her back and led her into the house.

***

Loretta marvelled as she entered the house. Ray took his time designing it to his taste. She'd been here once—the day he invited her to join him and celebrate. She was happy for him. She knew he was good at his job. He was finally getting the recognition he deserved.

"Do you want a drink?" Ray's voice hovered at her ear.

She stared at a portrait of his late parents' wedding, which hung at the centre of the wall in the living room. "No," she replied and pulled his body to hers.

He noticed the desire in her eyes and opted to take her to the bedroom, but she shook her head and pulled him down to the couch.

Ray fell helplessly, buried his head in-between her breasts, and smiled. She caressed his hair, began to undress him, and gasped when she removed his shirt. His body was well-toned and firm. He was in good shape. She caressed his thick biceps, and his muscle trembled from her touch.

Loretta trailed her lips across the thick muscles of his stomach and heard him groan.

He planted his hands on her waist and glided her body against his stiff shaft.

She sucked in her breath when she felt his erection. He removed his trousers, and she gasped as his solid length sprang free. Her fingers latched on it, and he became hard as granite. She stroked it from root to tip, knelt, and took all of it in her mouth. She sucked deep.

Ray let out a guttural moan and began to undress her. He removed her clothes and began to massage the soft flesh of her arching breasts, rolling the nipples between his fingertips.

Tears of pleasure filled her eyes, and she sucked him hard. He gently squeezed each of her breasts and explored every inch of her body with his palm. Heat flared within her, and she rose and captured his lips with her mouth. They kissed gently, and she savoured every inch of his mouth. She felt his fingers touch her between her legs and whimpered as he began caressing her swollen flesh.

Loretta closed her eyes and kissed him harder. He pushed two digits inside her, and her body trembled. She heard his ragged breathing and gasped when he laid her gently on the couch and placed his head between her legs. He parted her swollen lips and sucked gently with his lips.

"Ray!" she called his name, and he increased his effort, delving his tongue deeper into her.

He brought out his face a minute later, panting after savouring every part of her pleasure palace. "Are you on pills?"

She nodded. She needed him to sink his shaft inside her right now.

He placed his shaft at the entrance and pushed in. She moaned, and he thrust in deeper and began to fuck her harder and faster. They soon moved at a steady rhythm, and the intense lovemaking left her breathless.

He placed his lips on her right nipple and blew her mind as his shaft filled every inch of her. She held him tight as she approached the climax.

Ray increased his pace hitting the hilt each time he drove inside her.

When the explosion came, it shattered her senses. She held his face and covered it with soft kisses. He climaxed soon after, grunting as he spilt his seeds inside her. He carried her, and they lay on the thick, carpeted floor listening to each other's heartbeat.

Loretta held him tight, her love for him evident in her eyes.

Afterwards, Ray cleaned up and prepared dinner, which they ate before they finally slept.

CHAPTER TWENTY

Ray opened his eyes and felt Loretta's hand caressing his cheek. He smiled and kissed her forehead.

"Good morning, honey." Her soft voice caressed his ears.

He pulled her closer to his chest and observed her beautiful face. "I love you," he whispered in her ears.

"You are the best. I love you too."

"No matter how demanding our jobs are, we will make this work," he said.

She nodded in agreement.

A minute later, Loretta checked her phone and received a message from her secretary that she had a meeting with investors by 10 am. As she told Ray about it and her business plan, Ray's hands reached for his phone, where he placed it on his bedstand. He got it and switched it on. Two minutes later, the phone rang, and he picked it up.

"Jesus Christ, Ray. We've been calling you. Gideon is furious. We need you here. Where are you?"

Frank's voice hovered in his ears. Ray removed the thick bedsheet covering his body and sat straight on the bed. He listened, making Loretta wear a look of concern on her face.

"Honey, what is—"

Ray held his hand for her to keep quiet.

He became alert as he continued to listen. "Where? How did it happen?"

"At the second Niger Bridge in Onitsha. His name is Chijioke Okafor. He is a final-year student at Nnamdi Azikiwe University, Awka in Anambra State. He stays with his sister at Onitsha during the weekend. He jumped inside River Niger two days ago. We've pulled out his body. It's messy right here, Ray."

Ray clenched his jaw. "Oh no, not again."

He ended the call a minute later, and anger enveloped him. Many university students were dying under abnormal circumstances. He and his team needed to stop these occurrences before it became too late.

"Honey, what happened?" Loretta was concerned.

Ray gazed at her as he rose from the bed. "Sweetheart, I have to go. It's the university students' case. We have a new development. I will see you soon. Today's meeting with the investors will be a success."

She nodded and smiled.

He kissed her and went to the bathroom to brush and dress up. He left the room when he was done.

***

Onitsha

At noon, Ray stepped into the one-storey non-descript building at Awka Road, which the divisional police headquarters in Onitsha used as a morgue. Immediately after Ray left Loretta, he'd headed to the Nnamdi Azikiwe International Airport in Abuja, where he took a 10 am flight to Asaba Airport. Once he reached Asaba, a city that shared a boundary with Onitsha, he'd taken a cab that brought him to the morgue. There, he met Frank, whose face was corrugated with stress.

Ray held Frank's hand and took him aside. "Where is James Ibru?"

"He called and said he is on his way."

Ray exchanged a glance with his partner and narrowed his eyes. "Frank, you are tired. You need to rest."

Frank waved it off. "I'm alright. Follow me. I'll like you to meet someone."

Ray nodded. He followed Frank, and they met one of the local police officers. He was light-skinned, thin, and had a weather-beaten face.

"Ray, this is Sergeant Major Timothy Emezie. He was one of the people who fished the body from the River Niger," Frank said.

Ray and Sergeant Major Timothy greeted in a firm handshake.

"Officer, Frank told me this was a final year student of Nnamdi Azikiwe University in Awka. Is there any other thing we know about him?"

"His father, Simon Okafor, is the former Chief Justice of Appeal Court," Timothy said.

Ray allowed the words to sink in and said, "What if this is an accident? How do we know this is suicide?"

"He made a strange Kedochat post before he went missing, after which his body was discovered."

Ray narrowed his eyes. "I'd like to see it."

The Sergeant Major took out a smartphone and showed him the post with two thousand comments.

"Going back to my roots," Ray read it aloud. "It's strange."

"I thought so too," Frank said.

"Who contacted the police when he went missing?" Ray asked.

"His sister, Amarachi. She is a first-year student at the same university. She called us yesterday and raised the alarm. We tracked his phone's GPS chip and saw his phone on the second Niger Bridge, where he left it. She was with us in the vehicle. She showed us the Kedochat post and kept crying. I ordered our fishermen to search for his body. We deployed the boat, and they scouted the river for his corpse. We fished out his body after searching for three hours," Timothy said.

Ray took in Timothy's words and stared vacantly at the empty wall. Then, a moment later, he asked, "Where is the corpse?"

Timothy led him to a room where he met Dr Kenneth and three police officers.

He stepped close to the body, held the sheet with his fingers and uncovered the face.

The boy's eyes were closed, making him appear asleep. In his early twenties, he was young, and his dark-skinned face was spotless. No one would have known he died by drowning.

Ray fixed his gaze at the pathologist. "Doc, did you notice anything else about the corpse?"

Dr Kenneth shook his head. "Nothing is out of place. We will find out more after the autopsy."

Ray stared at Timothy. "Where is her sister?"

"She came here with us and has refused to go. She is outside the morgue."

Ray left the building to meet her.

CHAPTER TWENTY-ONE

When Ray stepped out of the morgue, he took a left and walked fast. Frank and Timothy followed him. He looked ahead and saw a young girl who sat on a metal chair close to the wall. Her hands covered her face as she sobbed.

When they approached, she rose, her eyes red and filled with tears. She was dark-skinned, tall, and slim, but the sorrow in her eyes made her look frail.

She stared at them, an unspoken question in her eyes.

Ray stepped closer to her and said, "Amarachi, my name is Ray Okon. I'm a DSS Agent. I'm working with the police on this case. We are so sorry for your loss. I can't imagine the pain you feel for losing your brother."

The girl's legs wobbled, and she leaned her body against the wall.

"Please, we just want to ask you a few questions," Ray said, and she nodded.

"You told the police that you stay with your brother here in Onitsha. Is that correct?"

She nodded.

"When did you first notice something strange about your brother's behaviour?"

"One month ago," she said. "Chijioke used to be lively, but suddenly he stopped and changed. He kept to himself. I didn't understand what was happening to him. I thought it was a phase which would soon pass. Now, I knew I was wrong."

"What about your parents? Are they aware of what happened?"

"My parents travelled out of the country. I've told them. They are deeply concerned. Because of this, they've cancelled their trip and will take the next flight to Nigeria."

"Did your brother receive any strange visitors recently, or was he sick?"

"No," Amarachi said matter-of-factly. "Chijioke stayed out of trouble. He didn't have many friends. He was a good young man. He was so kind and selfless. I don't know why this happened to him nor why he took his own life."

Ray gave her his card. "We will get to the root of this. Call me if there is any other thing you remember."

The moment Ray gave Amarachi his card, his phone rang, and he stepped out to answer it.

"Am I speaking to DSS Agent Ray Okon?" A deep voice said.

"Yes," Ray replied.

"I'm Roland Amaechi, a police inspector working in Nsukka. We have a new case here that fits the pattern of the case you are working on."

Ray became alert. "Go on."

"His name is Kenneth Udeze. Everyone in the University of Nigeria Nsukka Campus calls him

Ken. He drank a poisonous drink named Sniper and took his own life after leaving a Kedochat post."

Ray raised his eyebrow. "What did he write in the Kedochat post?"

"I'm sorry," the police officer said. "That's the exact words."

"Is he a final year student at the university? What else can you tell me about him?"

"No, he isn't, but he graduated from the same university. Ken was the manager of Leno's Palace, a popular big-budget restaurant with branches across Nigerian Universities. He was in charge of the UNN, Nsukka branch and was friends with most of the students in the school. Everyone knew Ken. It's safe to say his name has become synonymous with nightlife on Campus."

Ray remained quiet for a while. "I'm thinking about his Kedochat post. I wonder what he is sorry for."

"Sir, we'd like you to come to Nsukka. How soon can you be here? There is something we would like to show you."

Ray promised to call when he was on his way and ended the phone connection.

When he met Frank, he mentioned the new development. "Frank, I'd like you to meet with Amarachi's parents when they get to Onitsha. They may provide us with more information about their son. I'll be going to Nsukka right away."

Frank nodded. Ray shook hands with Timothy and promised to stay in touch. He punched numbers on his phone and arranged for transportation to take him to Nsukka.

CHAPTER TWENTY-TWO

Ray left Onitsha at 4 pm and reached Nsukka by 7 pm. It was a stressful journey made worse by the road in a terrible state of disrepair, starting from Ninth Mile, Enugu and ending at Opi Junction in Nsukka. He was grateful to the police at Onitsha, who assigned him a police cruiser and a driver. The man in his mid-forties struggled to make conversation with Ray during the journey.

Ray's mind was far away, filled with unanswered questions about the most bizarre case he'd faced in his career. When they arrived at Nsukka, he thanked the driver and alighted from the vehicle.

He asked a shop owner where to get accommodation, and the bear-faced man gave him directions.

It was late in the evening. Ray decided not to call Inspector Roland, whom he guessed would be home with his family.

He hailed a cab, got in and gave the address needed. He peered through the window as the scenery passed— banners of political candidates and the flyover at Nsukka Ogige Market. Then, at a bend in the road, a sign indicated the way to the University of Nigeria, Nsukka campus.

He took a mental note of his environment as the driver followed his direction and took him to Runtown Hotel at Odenigbo Street. The hotel was an old one-storey building with the architectural styles of the 1980s. The driver stopped in front of the gate.

Ray stepped out and gave him a huge tip.

He entered the building through its revolving door. In the lobby, he paid for a room and collected the key from the receptionist. When he got to his room, he opened the door, dropped his travel bag, and slumped on the bed. He fell asleep minutes later and had a restless sleep where he thought about the disturbing suicide deaths.

His ringing phone woke him up at 8 am. He puffed out air, feeling bad at waking up so late. He answered the call.

"Good morning, Ray. This is Inspector Roland Amaechi. I saw the message you sent. I hope you had a wonderful journey."

Ray wiped the sleep from his eyes and sat bolt upright. "Yes, I did. Thank you, Inspector."

"Let's meet at the police station by 9: 00 am. It's not far from your hotel."

"Alright, give me the direction."

Ray listened as the policeman talked. He ended the call a minute later and rose from his bed. He showered, dressed casually, and went downstairs to the hotel's restaurant, where he ate breakfast— tea and bread mixed with egg.

He checked the time and stepped out of the hotel when he was done. He flagged a cab that took him to the local police station. The moment he alighted from the vehicle, a tall police officer with a beer belly saw him and walked toward him. When he came closer, he extended his hand. "You are DSS Agent Ray Okon, I presume."

"Yes, and you are Roland Amaechi."

"You are correct."

After exchanging pleasantries, Ray went straight to the issue at hand. "Tell me more about the victim. When did it happen, and where?"

Roland shook his head, and his face took on a mournful glow. "Oh, poor Ken. He was popular here, especially at UNN, Nsukka campus. Ken was a good man and had a successful business. The students are weeping. No one knew why he took his own life. He died last morning in his room at Odenigwe."

"I'd like to see the Kedochat post he posted before he died."

Roland nodded and brought out his Techno Smartphone. He punched some keys on the keypad and showed Ray the screen.

Ray saw he was already on Ken's Kedochat timeline. He read the post, which had one simple sentence. "I'm sorry."

"An apology," Ray observed.

"It appears so."

"After saying he was sorry, he went ahead and took his own life."

The inspector shook his head. "It's terrible and heart-breaking."

Ray stared at him. "Why did you contact us? How did it relate to our case?"

Roland was silent for a while. Finally, he met Ray's gaze and said, "You will find out when I take you to his house. Let's go."

Ray followed him and entered the policeman's Mercedes, parked close to a tree. He turned the key in the ignition, started the car and drove into the busy Odenigwe Road. They passed low-rise buildings and reached the Odenigwe neighbourhood, where Ken lived five minutes later. With one glance at the place, Ray knew it was the students' neighbourhood.

"Ken lived here when he was a UNN student and chose to remain here even after graduating and starting his business. The students loved him. He was the symbol of social life on the campus," Roland said as if he'd figured out what Ray was thinking.

They drove through a dirt road, stopped before a gated compound, and alighted from the vehicle. They entered the marbled compound and climbed the stairs, which took them to Ken's apartment on the second floor. As they got close, Ray observed the door to the victim's room was open. Two men in police uniforms stepped out of the room.

They shook hands with Roland. He introduced Ray to them, and the police officers greeted the new visitor. Then, they stepped aside, allowing them to enter.

The moment they entered, the stench in the room hit Ray's nose. The place was a beehive of activities. A yellow tape ran across the door. Two crime scene technicians combed through the room, lifting the rug. Two men covered the body in a white sheet and carried it out.

The whole house had been ransacked. All the framed photographs on the wall had been removed and placed on the floor.

"What is going on here?" Ray asked.

"Let me show you what we found," Roland said.

He led Ray to the bedroom door. He spoke with one of the crime scene technicians and gently removed the tape to allow entry. They entered the bedroom. That room had also been torn apart.

"This is where things got scary." Roland's voice boomed.

Ray's gaze darted across the room and froze on the pictures and cardboard papers covering the wall. His legs wobbled. "Oh, my God."

CHAPTER TWENTY-THREE

Ray's eyes widened as he stared at pictures of the five final-year students who had committed suicide. Their names were written beside each of their photos. The last photograph and name posted on the wall were for the latest victim—Chijioke Okafor.

"From what I'm seeing here, this is a well-planned attack," Ray said.

"Yes," Roland said. "That's what it means."

At that moment, Ray's phone rang, and he answered it.

"Ray, I got information that you are at Nsukka. What's going on there?" his boss, Gideon Owolabi, asked.

Ray gave him a quick update. "Right now, sir, I'm inside Ken Udeze's room. He was the manager of Leno's Palace on the UNN Nsukka Campus. We've found that the deaths were not suicide but a well-planned attack."

"Go on."

"Right now, I'm looking at the names and pictures of all the victims we've investigated in this case."

"This is troubling. Keep me updated. I want to know everything you and the police find there."

"I will, sir."

When the call ended, Ray glanced at the bizarre wall and turned to leave the room.

"Ray, there is something else you need to know," Inspector Roland said.

Ray looked at him. "Go on."

Roland said, "Before he died, Ken stayed in a hotel downtown for two days. He didn't come out. No one knew what he did there."

"Where is the hotel located?"

"It's close to Opi Junction. Thirty minutes away."

Ray reached Holiday Hotel and Resorts at Opi thirty minutes later. He passed motorcycle riders and bus drivers seeking customers at the Opi Junction and a teenage boy wearing a Chelsea FC jersey and carrying a carton of bottled water. He collected one bottle of water, gave him a thousand Naira, and told him to keep the change.

He crossed to the other side of the road and entered the paved hotel premises.

In the lobby, he met the receptionist and showed his badge. He explained his mission and gave her a signed letter written by Inspector Roland. She read it and then nodded.

He stated Ken's room number, which the inspector had told him. She confirmed it, gave him the key, and smiled.

Ray thanked her and climbed the stairs to the second floor. As he approached the door to the room, he felt the hair at the nape of his neck rise. He brought out his Beretta and edged closer until he reached the door. He turned the handle just to make sure. It was locked. He brought out the key and unlocked it, then entered.

Ray observed the well-furnished room where Ken Udeze stayed while he was alive. A noise caught his attention, but before he could react, a young light-skinned woman pointed a gun at him. She wore a blood-red Osborn gown that complemented her stunning beauty. She had high cheekbones and piercing dark eyes, which made her look lethal.

Millions of questions ran through Ray's mind as he tried to figure out how to deal with this situation.

"Drop the gun and raise your hands where I can see them."

Ray dropped his gun on the floor and raised his hands.

"Who are you?" Her voice boomed across the room.

Ray fixed his gaze on her. "I'm DSS Agent Ray Okon. Who the hell are you?"

CHAPTER TWENTY-FOUR

"My name is Sarah Aderinsola. I'm a federal agent working with National Intelligence Agency." She stared at him and brought down the gun. "You've told me who you are, but that's not enough. Why are you here?"

Ray showed his badge. "I'm a member of the DSS Criminal Investigation Department. Currently, my team and I are working with the police on a case. I arrived here yesterday to follow up on a lead I got concerning the case. The lead involves the death of popular barman and manager of Leno's Palace, Ken Udeze, who allegedly committed suicide." Ray paused and stared at her as a serious expression appeared on her face. "What about you? What are you doing here? This is a federal investigation. You have no reason to be here."

"I'm a member of the NIA Cybersecurity Unit. We use intelligence gathering devices to detect threats to National Security and disable them at their infancy stage. I was sent undercover in Nsukka to get close to Ken and track his organization. Now, he is dead, and we are back to square one."

Ray raised his eyebrow. "What organization does he belong to? I—"

Sarah raised her hand and cut him off. "Wait. Why don't we do it this way? I give you Intel about my case, and you give me yours."

Ray shook his head. "I will only give you information that is public knowledge. Others are classified."

"Then forget about it. I'm leaving. It's nice meeting you, Ray." Sarah flashed him a smile and headed for the door.

Ray considered his options. "Wait!"

She turned.

"Alright," Ray said.

Sarah returned, and they sat on two plastic chairs in the room. She looked at Ray and said, "Tell me about the case you've been working on. What do you know about Ken Udeze?"

"My team and I are working on a case involving the death of final year university students. The evidence shows that they committed suicide. I arrived here yesterday to follow up on a lead. A member of the police force here informed me that Ken Udeze, the manager at Leno's Palace, had committed suicide. His death didn't fit the pattern, but I was taken aback when the police showed me names and pictures of all the five final years students that had died."

"How did you get to know about this place?" Sarah asked, her sharp eyes not missing a thing.

"One of the police office officers told me Ken spent two days in this hotel room before he died in his apartment at Odenigwe. I wanted to find out why." Ray broke eye contact with Sarah and stared at the wall. "It's been a bizarre ten days for us and the police. Five final-year students have died so far. Yet, we've not made headway in this case."

"How do you know it's suicide?"

"The police believed strongly they were suicides, but now I have my doubts, especially after seeing the names and pictures in Ken's bedroom. However, there seems to be evidence pointing to the students dying due to the high level of stress they faced in school. They also believe the victims were deeply affected by complicated life problems, which we discovered during the investigation that most of them had. There's more. They left weird suicide notes on their personal Kedochat pages before they died. That bothers me."

"What again did you discover?" Sarah asked.

"That's all we have right now. I've been trying to find out if there is anything that connects the victims that explains why they committed suicide. Do they belong to a cult group? Do they have enemies on campus? Etc. They were from different Nigerian Universities. The deaths appear to be random suicide deaths. But this new revelation shows it's a well-planned attack but by whom? There are still so many questions popping up."

Sarah stared at him for a moment and said in a low voice, "They are not random suicide deaths. What you saw in Ken's room shows something else going on here."

Ray narrowed his eyes as the muscles in his face tightened. "Why do you say so? I know I've told you about the names and pictures in Ken's room, but you sound like you know something about this case. Do you have any information about this case? We need all the help we can get." Ray remembered what Sarah told him earlier. "You said you've been working undercover, and the plan was to get close to Ken. Tell me about it."

"You've finally come to the point where it all connects," Sarah said.

Unanswered questions filled Ray's mind. "What do you mean?"

"The key to finding out what is going on and why these final year students are dying is in Leno's Place and the organization that owns them. We've been investigating them for the past nine months."

Ray's heart raced. They were getting close to finally unravelling this case. "Go on."

"From what you saw in Ken's room, you would discover that there is a list. Ken probably killed himself or was killed because of this organization's plans. Maybe he killed himself or was killed because he opted out. That's why he wrote 'I'm sorry' on his last Kedochat post."

Ray's eyes widened. Everything clicked and began to make sense. *Oh, God,* he thought.

"The deaths are not suicide. The students were targeted and killed. Everything was planned and executed to perfection. The deaths were made to look like suicide. The perfect crime. Who would ever doubt that? This organization has people on this list. They are killing them one by one. Right now, they have moved to the person who would become their next victim." She paused, staring at him with sad eyes. Her voice sounded like a punch in his ears. Stunned, his jaw dropped.

"Some people in this country have been marked to die." She turned, paced the room, and turned back to face him. "We are dealing with a ruthless enemy. We don't exactly know who they are or what their mission is. Right now, we have vague ideas about their identity. But, from the Intel we've gathered, they are planning something big. I believe that if both our agencies work together on this case, we will stop them."

Ray asked the questions on his mind since she started releasing the bombshell.

"What is the name of this organization? Who are they? Tell me everything you know about them."

CHAPTER TWENTY-FIVE

Gideon Owolabi sat impatiently in a big, upholstered chair in his double-windowed office in the Lagos DSS Branch Office Building. He tapped his hands anxiously on his mahogany desk and waited for Steve Maccido, the chief of the DSS Lagos Branch, to join him.

Sir, some people have been marked to die. What his agent, Ray Okon, told him on the phone two hours ago deeply unsettled him. This case had spiralled out of control. The media had started spinning conspiracy theories saying all kinds of things in the papers that were certainly not true. Bad news sells. He got it. The situation would worsen if they didn't get a handle on this soon.

Three days ago, journalists ambushed him when he was about to enter his office, asking him questions about the case. He told them the two agencies were working on it and would soon give them all the necessary information. Still, they weren't satisfied, and like hungry beasts, which they were, they used him to make headlines on the news, saying he told them he was in the dark concerning the case.

Gideon's jaw tightened, and he hit his fist on his desk. Threatening to sue them would make matters worse and make him and the agency look guilty. Already, his superiors were angry at him and had told him to set up a meeting with his people.

Ray had also told him about an NIA agent working undercover on a case connected to the University Students' Case.

Gideon checked the time. 10:15 am. At that moment, the door opened, and Steve entered. He shook hands with Gideon and took a seat next to his desk.

"Are we ready?" Steve asked him.

"Yes, we are."

"Great, let's begin," Steve said.

Gideon lifted the remote, and two big HD screens attached to the wall lit up.

Frank appeared on the first screen. Gideon knew he was still working with the police at Onitsha. Frank greeted him and Steve. They nodded. Ray and the NIA agent appeared forty-five seconds later, on the second screen, looking serious. Finally, the image of top DSS analyst Christine Zainab appeared on a small section of the screen.

"Welcome, everyone," Gideon spoke and looked at Ray. "Go ahead, Ray."

"Good day, sirs," Ray said and looked at the woman beside him. "This is Sarah Aderinsola. She is an agent from the Cyber Security Unit of the National Intelligence Agency. She has fresh information she would like to share with us concerning the case."

"Welcome, Sarah," Gideon said.

"Welcome, Sarah. I've heard great things about you. It's great to finally speak with you," Steve said.

A warm smile covered Sarah's face. "Thank you, sirs, for the warm welcome. I'm grateful."

"Go on, Ray," Gideon said.

Ray narrated the conversation he had with Sarah. "According to Sarah, the deaths were not by suicide. The students were murdered. Everything was professionally executed." He paused and continued, "Let me allow Sarah to take it from here."

He turned to Sarah.

"You are right, Ray," Sarah said and continued. "Our agency has been investigating the owners of Leno's Palace for the past nine months. We started after a new owner bought Leno's Palace, and we began to get reports that they participated in cyber-attacks and fraudulent activities. Six months ago, I began to work undercover at Leno's Palace, UNN, Nsukka Branch. My aim was to get close to Ken Udeze, the manager of Leno's Palace in Nsukka, who we suspected was a high-ranking member of the main organization. Since then, we've uncovered many things, but—"

Steve cut her off and asked, "What is the name of this organization?"

"Banzida Corporation. They are the owners of Leno's Palace. They also have a big tech company in Nigeria, Kenya, Ghana, and South Africa known as Esiris. It provides broadband, internet, and cloud computing services to businesses and web developers. Banzida is one of the few companies that provide such services in Africa."

Gideon stared at the other lady on the screen, DSS Analyst Christine Zainab. Ray brought her into DSS CID. She was efficient and results-driven. "Christine, what do we know about them?"

Christine sat in front of a laptop at her Abuja DSS CID workstation. She typed on the keyboard, and an elderly man appeared on the big screen. "Banzida was popular in the eighties. It was founded by Chief Bernard Oprokopa, now in his eighties. Apart from having a restaurant business, Banzida also had a construction and real estate business. A new company bought Banzida three years ago."

Gideon frowned. "I remember Banzida. Its founder Chief Bernard is a respected businessman honoured with the Order of the Niger by the previous administration. I'm not aware that he has sold his business."

"Who is the new owner of Banzida?" Steve asked.

Christine tapped on her keyboard. "Almost everything about the company's acquisition by the new owner was kept top-secret." She tapped the keyboard for a while and stared at the screen. "His name is Dominic Tiza. He is the new CEO of Banzida. Dominic acquired Banzida three years ago. However, I don't know if he is the only person that owns Banzida Corporation."

"Sarah, you mentioned Banzida engages in cyber-attacks and fraudulent financial activities. Do you have any evidence?" Gideon asked.

"We haven't gotten any evidence yet. Ken was about to reveal the information to me before he died," Sarah said."

Steve said, "Christine, tell us more about Leno's Palace. Where are they located?"

Christine stared at her computer screen and said, "Leno's Palace has branches in 180 tertiary institutions in Nigeria. They have become the favourite restaurant for children of the rich and undergraduates with deep pockets. Its new owner, Dominic Tiza, upgraded the services. Now, Leno's Palace has a website where students on each campus can order food online and receive it in their location within two hours. At the beginning of this year, Vanguard Newspaper rated them as the best restaurant business in the country. They have a strong online presence and a big office in Abuja."

Gideon shifted his attention to Ray. "Ray, you mentioned that you saw a list in Ken Udeze's room. You and Sarah said that some people have been marked to die. Who are these people? Are there more university students that have been marked to die?"

"We don't know yet, sir. We are working on finding out the identity of the people in this list," Ray said.

"Sarah, how does Banzida Corporation connect to the university students' case?" Frank asked.

"When I was an undercover agent at Leno's Place in Nsukka, I worked as a waitress in the restaurant. I made a breakthrough a month when I saved Ken's life. That night, he was almost attacked on a lonely road. I suspected something was wrong then and began to tail him. I shot the killer to death before he could kill Ken. Ken was surprised that his waitress knew how to use a gun. He asked me who I was, and I finally revealed my identity. I told him my mission and assured him that our agency would give him protection if he told us everything he knew. He was afraid but promised to talk to me when we agreed to give him immunity. The next time we met, he confirmed what we already knew about Banzida Organization."

"What's that?" Gideon asked, gritting his teeth.

"They are using Leno's Palace as a front for their illegal criminal activities. We agreed to meet on Monday, but he suddenly died two days ago.

"Was he killed?" Steve asked.

"I've been to Ken's room. It appears he was killed, and his death was made to look like suicide," Ray replied.

"This is serious," Frank said.

"There is something important you should know about the list of names in Ken's room," Sarah said, and everyone stared at her.

"Go on," Gideon said.

"I know it's easy to assume that Banzida would paste the list of names of people they've killed to show us they have a list. However, the Banzida we've been tracking for months is a very secretive organization. They are cautious and wouldn't want anything revealing their plans and stopping them from achieving their goal.

Remember, I said Ken told me we would meet. But he died before he could tell us the truth about Banzida."

"Yes, go on, Sarah," Gideon said.

"My gut tells me Ken knew he would die. I had already stopped Banzida's first planned attack on him, but he knew Banzida wanted to kill him. I believe he left the list there for me and the authorities. The list is his message to the authorities which reveals the crimes of Banzida."

"Oh, God. This makes sense," Ray said.

"Until now, we haven't found any direct evidence linking Banzida to any criminal activity, but we will."

Gideon scribbled something on his notepad and said, "Frank, liaise with the police and work with our analysts to find out the connection between the victims and why they were killed." He stared at Ray and Sarah and said, "I want both of you to question the deputy manager of Leno's Palace in UNN, Nsukka Campus. Find out everything we need to know about this organization. Unravel their plans and stop them before they do more harm. We will provide you with all the help and resources you need. I want daily updates."

"Yes, sir," they replied.

"Sarah, I will contact your superiors after this meeting to seek for our agencies to cooperate. We must share Intel and work together on this case."

Sarah nodded.

The meeting ended. Gideon pressed the remote on the wall, and the screen turned black. Gideon made a mental note to set up an appointment with NIA when everyone had left.

He tapped his fingers on the notepad and scribbled 'Banzida Corporation.' Next, he drew a circle around the name.

CHAPTER TWENTY-SIX

Cornelius Maduka, the deputy manager of Leno's Palace UNN Nsukka branch, stepped into the restaurant with renewed confidence at seven in the evening. He wore designer clothes and flashy shoes, which befitted his new status.

Leno's Palace was in a large one-storey building. The ceiling was decorated with chandeliers and blue lights. The tables were arranged to suit the expensive taste of their customers, who were children of the rich. Phyno's song, Connect, blared on the speakers.

Cornelius passed a male student who sat beside a pretty year-one female student, out on a date. *That's what they do*, he thought as he smiled. Leno's Palace was the perfect palace to impress a lady.

Neon lights shined at the entrance as he stepped out of the restaurant section and made his way to the VIP Lounge. The lounge was the symbol of nightlife on the campus. Heat flushed through Cornelius as he watched beautiful girls in sleeveless tops and tight-fitted miniskirts that revealed a little too much.

They ground their asses on the rigid members of their partners. A lady without a partner scanned the crowd looking for potential prey. As he moved through the group of people dancing and drinking Moet, he greeted familiar faces and shook hands with his friends. He was in a good mood tonight and would ensure he got laid.

Two hours earlier, he received a message from the headquarters. He'd been promoted to Manager of Leno's Palace in UNN after his boss, Ken Udeze, took his own life.

He had always admired Ken. It pained him that he had to die that way. He didn't want to think about it. That was in the past. He was the manager now. It meant a bigger pay-check and a chance to move out of his crappy one-room apartment at Opi Junction. His girlfriend Nancy had been complaining about it. He could move into a two-bedroom flat in GRA, Nsukka.

He walked in long strides and soon entered his new office. He closed the door and let his eyes take in the space. It was huge with a tiled floor and had a bookshelf that ran along the entire length of one wall. He had already set his MacBook Pro on the mahogany desk.

Cornelius crossed to the desk and sat on the black executive chair where Ken used to sit and give orders like an army general. *Now, a new general is in charge*, he thought as he smirked.

He took a deep breath and allowed himself to relax. Chilly air from the air conditioner close to his desk blew across his face, and joy flooded him. He booted up his laptop and logged into their branch's website. He watched the screen and saw three students placed orders for fried rice, chicken, salad, and canned Malt drinks. Cornelius processed the order and attached a bottle of Eva water each to their food. He hit send and got a note that it had been sent to the cash manager. The cash manager would process it and forward it to the logistics unit, who would deliver the food with their motorcycles. Everything had been optimized.

That made Leno's Palace unique, and their customers' money kept pouring into their restaurant's bank account. The UNN branch of Leno's Palace was the best performing branch last year. Cornelius intended to hit the same target this year. He had great plans and wanted to keep climbing the corporate ladder and eventually reach the top.

When he was done, he made a call.

"Congratulations, baby. I got your message," a sexy female voice boomed in his ears.

Cornelius smiled. "Thank you, sweetheart. I can't wait for us to celebrate tonight."

Nancy promised to spend the night with him, and he ended the call feeling satisfied.

At that moment, his door opened, and two people entered his office.

"Who is..." Cornelius stopped mid-sentence as he stared.

A tall, light-skinned woman of stunning beauty with piercing eyes who looked dangerous walked in with a dark-skinned athletic man in a black jacket and chinos who he guessed was five feet ten inches.

He guessed that both were in their thirties. There was something different about them. His heart raced, and his hand edged closer to a gun he kept next to him.

"I wouldn't advise you to do that, Cornelius," the lady said.

He stared at her as panic gripped him.

The man stepped closer to his desk. "Mr Cornelius Maduka, I'm DSS Agent Ray Okon. My partner's name is Sarah Aderinsola. We'd like to ask you some questions."

CHAPTER TWENTY-SEVEN

"Give me the gun," Ray ordered him.

Cornelius placed the gun on his desk and pushed it close to where Ray stood.

Ray collected it and wondered what else was happening at Leno's Palace. He figured Banzida Corporation might have bugged the entire place to keep an eye on their employees. He and Sarah exchanged glances. Finally, they led Cornelius out of the building. When Ray flagged a taxi, Sarah opened the passenger door for Cornelius and said, "Be quick. We don't have time."

"Why are you doing this? What is going on here?" Cornelius protested, but when he saw their faces, he entered the car. Sarah sat in the backseat beside Cornelius, and Ray sat in front beside the driver.

Once everyone had taken their seats in the car, the driver drove for twenty minutes while listening to Ray as he gave him directions. Then, as instructed, he stopped the vehicle by the roadside and cut the engine. Ray tipped the man hugely and whispered in the driver's ear, telling him to return an hour later for his vehicle. Nodding, the man stepped out of the car and walked away.

When the driver had left, Ray and Sarah alighted from the vehicle. Then, Sarah opened the passenger door and dragged Cornelius out of the car.

Ray stared at him. "Why are you in possession of a gun? This is enough to send you to prison."

Cornelius's hands trembled. "This is a rough neighbourhood. Cultists, most of whom are students, frequent Leno's Palace at night. I use it for protection. I'm sorry. I—"

"If you give us the information we need, we will not arrest you for illegal possession of a firearm," Sarah said.

"Yes, you've heard what Sarah said. Just give us the information we need, and we will allow you to go."

A worried look appeared on Cornelius's face. "What do you want? I don't know why you are doing this. We are doing legal business at Leno's Palace. We don't engage in any illegal activities, and we pay our taxes to the government."

"What happened to Ken Udeze? Was he killed by your organization?" Ray asked.

"No, of course not."

"You work for Banzida. Tell us everything you know about Banzida and your CEO, Dominic Tiza," Sarah said.

Ray watched for micro-expression, catching a hint of fear on Cornelius's face.

"Oh, no. We are completely legal. What I know about Banzida is the same thing written on our company's official website. Banzida is a huge corporation with different sectors and departments.

I only know about one of its businesses—Leno's Palace. I can tell you how we operate. You are free to look at our record books. We—"

Ray cut in. "Did you notice anything suspicious that happened a few days before Ken died? Think, you may remember something."

Cornelius shook his head. "None at all. I'm telling you the truth."

Ray brought out his phone. "I will call the police if you don't start talking. If you keep giving us these scripted speeches, we will arrest you for illegal possession of a firearm and hand you over to the police."

"They will put you in prison, where you will rot in jail for the rest of your life. All your hopes and dreams will be crushed," Sarah added.

Cornelius's hands continued to tremble. He looked down and stared at the ground.

Ray fixed his stern gaze at him and said, "Let me ask you for the last time. A few days before Ken died, did you notice anything strange? Did anyone pay him a visit in your office?"

"Okay, I'll tell you what I know. Please, I don't want to go to jail," Cornelius pleaded, his eyes darting right and left.

"Go ahead," Sarah said.

"Two men visited Ken a day before he died. I thought it was strange. They were high-ranking members of Banzida Corporation. I'd never seen it happen before."

"Where did this meeting take place?" Sarah asked.

"Right inside his office. I knew because Ken called me and asked me to get them drinks. When I came back, there was fear in his eyes. I've never seen that expression on his face. I was concerned. The next day, he died. A part of me told me something was terribly wrong, but I kept my thoughts to myself."

Ray asked, "Who are they?"

"Right now, I remember only the identity of one of the men."

"Who is he?"

"His name is Lucas Mordi. He is the manager of Leno's Palace at the University of Ibadan."

Ray put his phone to his ear to speak with Frank. At that moment, they heard an approaching vehicle. Ray saw it was a police cruiser. It drove closer to where they stood and stopped beside them. The car door flung open, and Inspector Roland and two policemen alighted.

Inspector Roland collected the gun, and one of his men dragged Cornelius against the body of the taxi and handcuffed him. "Mr Cornelius Maduka, you are under arrest for the illegal possession of a firearm."

Ray had texted Roland earlier to come with his men to their location.

As the men dragged Cornelius to the vehicle, he looked back and said to Ray, "But sir, you said you will not arrest me."

"You broke the law, and you have not told us everything you know."

As Cornelius entered the police cruiser, Ray and his partner walked away.

He made calls, and Frank arranged a helicopter to take him and Sarah to Ibadan.

CHAPTER TWENTY-EIGHT

Ray and Sarah arrived in Ibadan the next day at 4 pm. They got accommodation at Princeton Hotel close to the University of Ibadan. Both lodged in rooms close to each other. The clouds were dark, and a few minutes later, rain poured down. Ray sat on a chair in his hotel room and scribbled essential details on his notepad.

Sarah was in her room. She'd looked exhausted, and he'd advised her to get some sleep. He didn't want to disturb her.

When he was through, he called Frank. "Thank you so much, Frank, for asking Onitsha police to use their helicopter to ferry us to Ibadan. We are grateful. We have arrived and have lodged in a hotel."

"It's nothing, Ray. It's important that we move fast on this case."

"We will locate the Lucas Mordi tomorrow."

"Keep me updated."

"I will," Ray said and ended the call.

Ray rose and headed straight to the window. He was on the third floor of the hotel. His room allowed him to see the beautiful landscape of the city. Next to the hotel was the University of Ibadan, one of the oldest universities in Nigeria.

Ahead was the Trans-amusement Park building, which was close to Surulere Street and the famous Bodija Market.

The rain had reduced to a drizzle. The weather was cold and everywhere was calm. Ray loved the stillness. It allowed him to think.

He returned to the desk and scribbled the name 'Lucas Mordi' on his notepad. *What did you do, Lucas? Where are you right now?* He rose and ambled to his bed. He released his weight on the king-size bed and fell asleep soon afterwards.

He woke up by six a.m. the following morning, brushed his teeth, and did a hundred push-ups which helped him to stay fit. Afterwards, he showered and ordered food from room service.

He texted Sarah.

Ray: *Are you ready?*"

Sarah: *Yes.*

They had agreed to leave by 8 am. Both didn't want to contact the police. They had decided to keep their visit a secret.

Ray dressed up and stepped out of the room with his Beretta. He knocked at Sarah's door, and it opened a minute later. She stepped out, and both walked out of the hotel.

He made a call to a car hiring company. Frank had given him the number. He mentioned his location, and one of their drivers arrived with a BMW fifteen minutes later. He paid the chubby fortyish driver, who gave him the key and left. When Ray and Sarah got into the car, he pressed Christine's number and put the call on speaker.

She picked on the second ring. "Good day, sir," came her voice.

"Hi, Christine. We are at Ibadan now. Sarah is here with me."

"Hi, Sarah." Christine's voice carried her usual excitement.

Sarah greeted her back. After the exchange of pleasantries, Ray said, "Where is Lucas now?"

"He is in Ibadan. Let me check...." He heard her typing fast on the keyboard.

"Right now, Lucas Mordi is inside the University of Ibadan. He is at Barth Road."

Ray started the engine, punched the location in the car's GPS, and drove off.

***

Ray arrived at the University of Ibadan and drove to Barth Road, where Kenneth Dike Library was located. Christine called and told him that Lucas was at the university's first gate. So, he headed down there.

When he got there, he didn't see him. He stopped, lowered his driver's window, and said to one of the security men at the gate, "Good day, sir. I have a meeting with Lucas, the manager of Leno's Palace here. I have been calling him, but the call is not going through. I—"

"You mean Lucas Mordi," the security man asked. The middle-aged man was dark, and his face was full of dark spots.

"Yes."

"You just missed his blue Mercedes." He gazed across the road and pointed toward a vehicle that slowed down at Agbowo Road. "Oh, see him."

Ray and Sarah saw him. Ray thanked the man and drove the car to Agbowo Road. He followed Lucas at a distance. Lucas took a right, and Ray thought he was returning to the campus.

He entered Akintobi street and then drove into Old Oyo Road. Ray followed him and maintained the distance. Five minutes later, both were held by a red traffic light and had to stop. Ray's eyes narrowed when Lucas ignored the red light and suddenly drove fast.

"He knows," Sarah said.

Ray took off after him.

CHAPTER TWENTY-NINE

Ray chased Lucas, dodging vehicles, and almost hitting a motorcycle rider. When they got to Mokola roundabout, he saw a narrow opportunity and took it. A truck came from the opposite direction, heading towards Lucas's vehicle. Lucas slowed and moved to the left side of the road. Ray gunned the engine and moved to the other side of the road. He overtook Lucas and blocked him.

Suddenly, Lucas quickly reversed, took a right, and entered Sabo Road.

"He's running," Sarah shouted.

Ray followed him while gripping the steering wheel firmly. He dodged a Toyota vehicle and entered Sabo Road. He drove faster and closed the distance between them. As Lucas entered Onireke Road, Ray withdrew his gun and shot the car's back tyre through the window. Sarah brought out her Glock and pulled the trigger. Her bullet shattered the car's back windscreen. Ray's bullet hit the second tire. He watched as Lucas drove without control until he crashed his car into a tree.

Ray and Sarah quickly alighted from their vehicle and rushed to Lucas's car. Both were alert as they watched him climb out of the wreckage.

Ray got there first and dragged him out. Sarah kicked him hard.

He handcuffed him and stared at him. Lucas appeared to be in his early thirties. His eyes were red, and he smelled of beer.

Ray flashed his badge. "Lucas Mordi, you visited Ken Udeze at his office in Leno's Palace in UNN, Nsukka campus, a day before he died. Did you kill him or poison him? We saw a list which was pasted on the wall of his room. Who are the people on the list?"

"What is Banzida planning?" Sarah asked.

Lucas spat out blood. Ray observed as hate filled his eyes, and he kept mute.

"You only have one chance to tell us what we need to know, or you will spend the rest of your life in Kiri Kiri prison."

"Go to hell," Lucas muttered.

"Ray's eyes widened. "What?"

Lucas met Ray's gaze and smiled. "You will never know. You can't stop us."

"You are..." Ray stopped in midsentence when he saw Sarah move fast and place her hands on Lucas' face.

She struggled to pry his mouth open. His body shook as though he was having an attack. First, he trembled violently, and then his body became still.

Sarah rose and glanced at Ray, her eyes showing her exhaustion. "He probably took cyanide and killed himself."

Ray clenched his jaw.

"Ray, this is serious. Whatever Banzida and their people are planning, they are willing to die for it."

CHAPTER THIRTY

Ray spoke with James Ibru and told him about Lucas Mordi. James connected him to Jim Onibonjo, the deputy commissioner of police in Oyo State Police Command. In thirty minutes, police sirens filled their ears as three cruisers arrived. They asked Ray questions about what happened. He gave them a summary of how Lucas died, removing parts he didn't want them to know.

They took Lucas's corpse, loaded it inside a transport van and drove off after that.

Ray pressed the number he knew by heart. Christine picked on the first ring.

"Christine, I want you to check where Lucas lived."

"Alright, sir. Give me a moment."

She called back three minutes later and said, "I searched the FRSC database and got the information from his driver's license. Lucas Mordi lived in the Agbowo neighbourhood."

"We moved past Agbowo. It's close to the first gate of the University of Ibadan," Sarah commented.

Ray nodded and said, "Thank you, Christine."

He ended the call.

They got into their vehicles, and Ray drove to Agbowo. When he entered Agbowo, he saw many people inside Bet Naija shops that filled the area. Some of the women hawked foodstuffs. He guessed they wanted easy money and decided to try their hands on sports betting.

Ray took a tiny dirt road filled with water and drove slowly. Mud and old buildings littered the street. Students rushed to lectures, and others smoked weed on the balcony of an old three-storey building.

"My aunt lives here in Ibadan. I once stayed with her during the holiday when I was still in school. She warned me not to go to this neighbourhood."

"Why?" Ray asked, but from what he'd observed, he knew the answer.

"Agbowo is a hotbed of crime. It is filled with cultists, pickpockets, and thieves. It's a very dangerous place for anyone, including students, to live," Sarah explained.

It is obvious, Ray thought as his left hand tightened on his gun.

He stopped a young lady with a black handbag he assumed was a university student. "Where does Lucas Mordi—the manager of Leno's Palace live?"

"Oh, you are close," the student said. "Continue to go straight. When you reach the end of the road, go right, you will see his house. It is a white building."

Ray thanked her and drove off. When he saw the white building, he knew he was at the right place. He parked the car close to the black gate, and both he and Sarah alighted from the vehicle.

Lucas lived in a duplex. The building was fenced with an electric barricade and gated to ward off hoodlums. Ray pushed his hand through the hole in the pedestrian entrance and unbolted it. He shoved it, and they entered.

Ray observed three cars parked at different sides of the compound. Lucas lived there with his family. It was apparent to him that the luxury he saw there was a bit of a stretch for a restaurant manager. Where did he get all that money?

The moment they got close to the house, the front door opened, and a young, dark, and beautiful woman came out and fixed her angry gaze on them.

She blocked the door and was ready to bite. "Who are you, and what are you doing in my house?"

They showed her their badges and explained who they were.

"Madam, show us Lucas's room," Ray said.

"Where is your search warrant?"

Sarah glared at her. "If you delay for another minute, we will get it and then come back here with policemen and women from Oyo State Police Command."

"And if you obstruct a federal investigation, we will arrest you as one of his accomplices," Ray chipped in.

The lioness trembled and shifted to the side for them to enter the room. Once inside, they climbed the stairs, and she directed them to her husband's room. They entered the room, and Ray took in the scene in front of him. The master bedroom was furnished with heavy furniture and a navy-blue carpet. It was large and looked like a penthouse suit.

Sarah walked to the desk, brushed aside the wife's makeup kit, and looked at the content on the table. Ray dismissed the woman, and they began searching the room to find anything connecting Lucas to Banzida's plans. They searched the room for three hours and found a safe inside a backdoor. The safe was in the wardrobe and had a large lock. As Ray wanted to find out how to unlock it, Sarah pointed her gun at the safe and pulled the trigger, blowing the lock apart. The gunshot shook the entire house.

He met Sarah's gaze and signalled for her to be cautious next time. She waved it off and said, "Ray, take a look at this."

Ray rushed to her side. They saw a tiny notebook and brought it out. Sarah flipped through the pages with care. As she did that, a small piece of paper slipped from the pages and fell on the carpeted floor. Ray's hand reached for it, and he collected it.

He stared at the name written on the paper. "Gaius Abada."

He and Sarah exchanged a suspicious glance.

Ray brought out his phone and called Christine. She picked on the first ring. "Ray, where are you guys?"

Ray noticed the concern in her voice. "We are in Lucas's bedroom. Please, run a check for me. The name is Gaius Abada."

"Right away, sir."

The call ended.

The phone rang five minutes later, and Ray picked up the call.

"Gaius Abada is the son of the former Inspector General of Police, Stephen Abada. He studied Medicine and Surgery at Harvard University in the United States. He recently returned to Nigeria to do his National Youth Service Corps where he would join other fresh graduates to serve the country for a year as stated in the constitution."

"Where is he now?" Sarah asked.

"A second, please," Christine said, her voice breaking due to poor network.

"Right now, he is at the University of Abuja," she replied.

"Oh, my God," Sarah muttered.

"He is next," Ray said, reading her thoughts.

They dropped the search and walked out of the room.

CHAPTER THIRTY-ONE

Ray and Sarah rushed to Ibadan airport and took the next flight to Abuja. When the Ibom Air aircraft landed at Nnamdi Azikiwe International airport, Abuja, they disembarked and saw that the DSS had provided a Sienna vehicle. When the driver opted to take them to Gwagwalada, where the University of Abuja was located, Ray said, "Thank you, your job is done."

The driver left. Ray got into the driver's seat while Sarah sat beside him. He gunned the engine, and the vehicle hit the traffic lane. They were behind schedule and needed to move fast.

Gaius Abada, the boy's name, was on Ray's mind as he drove past the busy Abuja roads. When they got to the University, they saw many cars in front of the main gate. Most of them were police vehicles. The gathered crowd wore mournful looks.

Concerned, Ray parked the car beside the road, and both got out.

"What is going on?" he asked a policewoman who was of average height.

"It's Gaius Abada." She stared at them. "Do you know him?"

Ray became alert. "Yes, he is the son of the former Inspector General of Police, Stephen Abada."

"He visited a friend who is a student at this university during the weekend. He had just graduated from Harvard. He died yesterday. The sad thing is that he was just twenty-one years old," she said as Ray's eyes widened.

"What happened to him?" Sarah asked,

"We don't know much yet, but the doctors at the University of Abuja teaching hospital have ruled it as suicide. The whole thing is strange. This morning, the police arrested the student Gaius was staying with."

"What is his name, and where does he stay?" Ray asked.

"His name is Daniel. He is an undergraduate at this university. His apartment is in a building close to the gate."

"Where?" Sarah asked.

She pointed straight ahead. "Go straight and enter the road by the left."

They thanked her and got into the Sienna.

Daniel lived in an apartment in a three-storey building. When they arrived, six police vans and a crime scene van had walled off the house from the main road. The place was filled with law enforcement agents and reporters whose photographers took pictures every minute. A yellow tape covered the room's front door on the first floor where Gaius died.

Ray flashed his badge explaining who they were and asked to see the officer in charge. A policeman introduced them to another uniformed slim dark man in his early sixties. He was barking orders to his men when Ray and Sarah met him. Ray read his name on the tag attached to his shoulder: Menzi Abubakar.

The policeman who introduced them to him had already told them that Menzi was the chief superintendent of police.

Menzi was busy and did not want to be interrupted. However, he eventually turned to them. "One minute, what do you want?"

"We would like to ask Daniel a few questions. It is critical to the nationwide investigation we have been making on this case."

Menzi was quiet for a moment before he replied, "Daniel is not here."

"Where is he, sir?" Sarah asked.

"He is in detention at FCT Police Command Headquarters."

Ray thanked him, and they got into the car.

Thankfully for Ray and Sarah, the roads were clear. They got to Federal Capital Territory Police Command headquarters in Garki in forty-five minutes.

The two agents crossed a compulsory security check. After police officers confirmed their identity, they were permitted to see Daniel.

Ray and Sarah followed a short, chubby policewoman who took them to a three-storey building and led them to a police cell where Daniel was held.

She unlocked the door, said, "Five minutes," and then left.

The first thing Ray saw when they entered the room was a security camera placed at the top right side of the room. The room was painted white. Daniel sat on a chair, and his hands were chained to the metal table. Sweat covered his face. When he saw them, panic entered his eyes.

"Hello, Daniel," Ray greeted him as he brought a chair and sat close to the young undergraduate. Sarah sat beside him.

"My name is Ray Okon. This is my partner, Sarah Aderinsola. We are both federal agents involved in a nationwide criminal investigation."

"We would like to ask you a few questions about your friend, Gaius," Sarah added.

When Daniel heard the name, a flicker of pain appeared in his eyes.

"How do you know Gaius?" Ray asked.

"We were classmates in secondary school. He recently graduated. He was preparing for NYSC and came during the weekend to visit me."

"Are you a student at this university?" Sarah asked.

"Yes, I am a final year student of Medical Radiography," he answered and pleaded, "Please, I did not kill him. Gaius was a very good friend to me, and I would never do anything to harm him."

Ray was not moved by Daniel's theatrics. "You did not kill him. What happened to him? He died in your apartment when he came to spend the weekend with you," Ray said, losing his patience.

"Gaius left a Kedochat post before he died. I left the house early yesterday morning to go to church. When I came back, I was shocked when I saw him lying dead on the floor. I think he committed suicide. I rushed him to the University Teaching Hospital. The doctors declared him dead and reported me to the police. The police didn't want to hear what I had to say. They arrested me."

"Can we see the Kedochat post?" Sarah asked.

Daniel was not with a smartphone. Sarah brought out hers and opened the Kedochat app. He gave her the name of Gaius' Kedochat profile. She clicked it and scrolled till she got to the last post Gaius had made. She read it. "It is over."

The post had sad face emojis and over one thousand comments. As they continued to question Daniel, Ray's phone rang. He pulled out the phone from his trouser pocket and stared at the screen. It was Inspector Roland of Nsukka Police. He wondered why he was calling.

"Good day, Inspector Roland."

"Hi, Ray. Cornelius told me he remembered something. It is vital to the investigation," Roland said.

Ray stood, alert. Sarah came closer to him.

"Tell me about it," Ray said.

"He said the second man that came to visit Ken is Raman Abdul," the inspector replied.

"Raman Abdul." Ray said, "Who is he?"

When Sarah heard the name, curiosity appeared in her eyes.

"He is the manager of Leno's Palace at Ado Bayero University, Kano," Inspector Roland said.

At that moment, Ray had a terrible feeling. What was it about the managers of Leno's Palace?

However, he kept his thought to himself, thanked Roland, and ended the call.

He briefed Sarah about the call when they stepped out of the building after thanking the officers they greeted earlier. He wanted to make a call and arrange for transportation, but Sarah raised her hand.

She joined him after making a phone call. "That's not necessary. I have called my boss at National Intelligence Agency. We've investigated Raman for financial fraud for years but have not gotten any evidence to tie him to the crime. Now, we are so close to catching him. My boss told us to come to the airport. A jet is waiting to fly us to Ado Bayero University in Kano."

CHAPTER THIRTY-TWO

The flight to Kano took forty minutes. Ray wished they'd gotten there sooner. When their jet landed at an empty stadium at Ado Bayero University, they entered a vehicle arranged by DSS, waiting for them at the stadium.

"Where to?" asked Ahmed, the dark-skinned driver in his early forties.

"Take us to Leno's Palace," Ray said.

"Oh, Leno's Palace. The big man's restaurant. I know the place," the driver said. "What are you doing in Kano? I hope you like what you have seen so far. Kano is a historic city."

Ahmed continued to talk, but they kept silent. He drove past three female hostels and stopped in front of a big red building. An electric banner—Leno's Palace, Comfort redefined—was mounted atop the building.

"Wait here," Ray said to the driver as he and Sarah alighted from the vehicle.

A crowd had formed in front of the restaurant. Most of them were crying. Others spoke in the Hausa language. Ray didn't know what they were saying, but their faces showed they were sad.

Sarah told Ray to stop when they got in front of a sobbing lady. She wore Leno's Palace Uniform.

Ray guessed she was a cook at the restaurant. He greeted her and said, "Where is Raman?"

She stared at him, "You don't know?"

"What?"

"Our manager had an accident," she said.

"Where is he?" Ray asked.

"He is in Aminu Kano Hospital."

As they were about to leave, Ray asked her, "What is your name?" and told her who they were.

"Hadiza," she replied.

Ray gave her his card. "Call your number for me."

She called her digits, and Ray saved them on his phone. "We will call you if we need anything or any information from you."

She nodded and left.

Ray and Sarah rushed back to the car.

***

Aminu Kano Hospital was a large government hospital in the centre of Kano City. Cars and humans struggled for the small space between the gate and the main building. When Ahmed stopped the vehicle, both agents climbed out and rushed into the hospital. They stopped a nurse in a blue tunic.

"We are looking for Raman Abdul," Ray said.

"He had an accident. He was recently rushed to this hospital," Sarah added.

The nurse said, "Emergency room. Third floor. Room 301."

They hit the stairs, and once they got to the room, they saw two doctors leaving and stopped a nurse rushing to leave.

Ray approached her. "Excuse me. We are looking for Raman Abdul. A nurse told us he is staying here."

"I am sorry, we couldn't save him. He lost a lot of blood. By the time they brought him here, it was already late." She paused and gazed at them. "His corpse is not here. It's in the morgue. Are you his relatives?"

Both rushed out of the hospital. When they got back into the car, Ray gave Ahmed a bundle of naira notes and dismissed him. He did not want another set of ears hearing about the investigation. As he gripped the steering wheel, exhaustion crawled through his body.

"Back to square one," Sarah muttered.

Ray hit his head on the steering. When he raised his head, he turned to face Sarah and said, "We need to find out where he lived."

Sarah nodded in confirmation.

Ray called Hadiza. She picked on the second ring.

"Hadiza, this is Ray. Where does Raman live?" He could still hear her stifled sobs.

"You've gone to the hospital, right?" she asked.

"Yes."

"Raman is dead. It's so hard to believe he is gone. He was so good to us and made sure our salary was paid on time."

Ray could feel her pain. "I am so sorry for your loss." Then he asked, "How did the accident happen?"

"A huge truck knocked him out of the road in Baguda flyover as he was coming to Leno's Palace this morning. By the time people got there, the truck driver had disappeared. Raman was rushed to the hospital where he died."

"We will find out who did this," Ray promised her.

"Raman lived in Number 30 Katsina Road. It is close to Airport Road."

Ray thanked her and ended the call.

When they got to Raman's house, it was already filled with people. Two policemen sat in the sitting room questioning two women who Ray guessed were his wives. Five people consoled the two women.

Ray flashed his badge as he spoke to the policeman briefly who protested at their request. They gave him a number, and he called James Ibru. When the call ended, he said to the two agents, "Go ahead. Be quick. More family members will soon be here."

Ray and Sarah followed a long passageway and searched the rooms. When they entered the last room, Ray knew he was in Raman's study. They saw a laptop which sat on a huge desk. Ray booted it up. "It's locked."

"Let me take it from here," Sarah suggested.

Ray remembered she was a cyber security expert. "Alright."

He watched her for twenty minutes. She spoke with a colleague at her NIA office in Lagos as she worked.

"Done," she said.

Ray rushed to her side and observed that she had unlocked the laptop. They watched the screen as it showed Windows Ten. Sarah opened the Google Chrome Browser on the taskbar and checked for recent search history.

She opened the last website Raman visited. The website loaded and requested a login code. Its background was dark.

She read the website address. "www.cr.kt."

"What is that?"

"A website," Sarah said. She typed fast and hit send. "It's an encrypted network protected by a password."

As she typed fast on the keyboard, Ray went to look at the rest of the room. His eyes caught a huge painting on the wall. It was the picture of a big black bull pulling down a skyscraper building.

"Ray."

He stopped. Sarah's voice was tense. He rushed to her side and stared at the letter on the screen.

XX/X

"Twenty slash ten," she said. 'It could be anything. This is like looking for the needle in a haystack." Her voice showed she was tired.

Ray took a moment to think. He brought out his phone and checked the date. October twentieth. "Twenty is for the day, ten is for the month," he muttered.

Sarah gazed at him. Confusion lined her face. "What?"

"Twentieth day of October," he said.

Sarah stared at him as if he wasn't making sense. "You mean it's a date?"

"Yes, my guts tell me so."

They remained silent for a long moment until he broke the silence. "What significant thing took place on the twentieth of October?"

Sarah tapped the key as she searched through Google, "In which year?"

"Wait." A prominent result filled the screen. "Oh my God, 20th October 2018 was the day of the unpopular Bendi killings."

"An incident that happened four years ago during the ENDTACS protest," Ray added.

Sarah raised her head. "Yes, it is obvious. Banzida is planning something on this date."

CHAPTER THIRTY-THREE

When more mourners entered the house, Ray and Sarah didn't want to wait further. They took the laptop, greeted the officer, and walked out of the building. They were not finished with the computer yet. Sarah believed they could unravel the evidence tying Banzida to the crime through the laptop. And more, it was likely that they would find out what Banzida was planning. Ray agreed.

When they got into the car, he drove straight to Sani Abacha Road and stopped in front of a four-star hotel. The hotel was five stories high, and its walls were covered with tiles.

The door opened automatically as they got close, and they entered. Ray paid for two rooms to the receptionist in the lobby.

"How many days?" the receptionist asked.

"We may stay for a day but make it one week."

The young man pressed his keyboard and gave them a receipt from the printer. He gave Ray the two keys. "Room 201 and 202. Both are on the second floor."

Ray thanked him, and they climbed the stairs. Their rooms were close to each other. Sarah collected her key and the laptop and entered her room when they got there.

Ray got into his room, closed the door, and collapsed on the huge bed. The room was big. It had a fantastic view showing the beauty of the historic city. Sarah would be working on the laptop and communicating with her colleagues. He hoped to hear the good news soon.

He rested and woke up twenty minutes later when his phone beeped. He brought it out and saw a message from Loretta. He'd texted her earlier and told her that he was in Kano.

Loretta: *Baby, you work so hard. Try and get some sleep.*

Ray: *I'm doing so now.*

They chatted about her work. Her business was going great, and he was happy for her. She had told him earlier that her meeting with the investors was successful. He wished her well and dropped his phone on the bedstand.

He tried to close his eyes again, but his gut told him he was missing something important. He couldn't sleep. He was restless. He tossed and turned in bed, his mind plunging him back to the case without permission.

"What was Banzida planning on twentieth October?" The question plagued his mind.

He heard a sound, and his hand quickly went to the gun strapped on his belt. It was probably nothing. He took a deep breath and tried to relax. He rested his head on the pillow as the frigid air from the air-conditioner blasted against his skin. He smiled, enjoying it.

Suddenly, he rose out of pure instinct, took his phone and gun, and rushed out of the room. He knocked on the door of Sarah's room. "Sarah, it's me. Open the door!"

"Ray, I'm busy. I'm unearthing damning things from the laptop. I need an hour, please," Sarah said from inside the room.

"Sarah, stop everything you are doing. Let's go!"

Five seconds later, the door opened, and her face appeared. She'd noticed the urgency in his voice.

"What? Where?"

Ray held her hand and dragged her out of the room. "Run."

They ran out of the building and dived across the road. A second later, the building blew up in an ear-shattering bang, and the debris hit them.

"Oh my God," Sarah said, her voice filled with panic. "They wanted to kill us." She paused for a moment and stared at Ray. "The laptop. The evidence!"

Ray held her hand. "Forget about it. It's gone. It is clear they wanted to kill us. They have only succeeded in destroying the evidence."

Now, Banzida Corporation was on their trail. They were the obstacle in their way. If Banzida had succeeded in killing them, they would carry out their plans on October twentieth. The thought disturbed Ray.

A new thought hit his mind. If Banzida was willing to go to this length to destroy evidence and kill them, it meant whatever the group was planning was far more dangerous than they'd imagined.

"It's not safe here. Let's go," Ray shouted.

Clothes torn and dirty, he dragged Sarah up, and they ran.

CHAPTER THIRTY-FOUR

The office building of Banzida Corporation in Abuja was architectural wizardry. It was twenty-one stories high. The walls were tiled, and the white structure was controlled by electricity, motion sensors, and shiny tech gadgets. Esiris—a tech company owned by Banzida Corporation, took the entire top five floors of the skyscraper building.

Dominic Tiza, the chief executive officer of Banzida, sat behind a transparent desk inside his plush twenty-foot office on the twenty-first floor of the building. His intense eyes blazed with anger as he typed fast on his laptop, working on a new 5G program his team had developed for Esiris.

Thirty-five years old, he was dark-skinned with a thick chest and rippling muscles. A deep scar ran across his right chest.

Banzida Corporation had four different businesses. First was Leno's Palace, the modern-day restaurant spread across Nigerian universities. Its revenue had broken records since Dominic took over Banzida three years earlier. Secondly was Ladoo, a real estate company. Thirdly was Banzida Construction Firm. The fourth and the last was Dominic's brainchild—Esiris.

Dominic officially registered Esiris as a business fifteen years ago. Within the last decade, it had edged ahead of its local competitors, becoming one of the fastest-growing tech companies in Africa. After acquiring Banzida, he merged Esiris with the rest of Banzida Corporation three years ago. That year, Forbes Magazine named him Africa's youngest billionaire.

Esiris was a tech company that developed innovative software, broadband technology and provided internet services to businesses across the continent. Its data centre—the largest in West Africa—was based in Ghana. Esiris became the first African tech company to roll out its broadband technology nine years ago and was now the largest in Africa.

Dominic's office was huge and oval-shaped. His desk, electric wheelchair, and a sofa sat at the centre of the office. Everything could be pulled up with the hit of a button. Dominic had succeeded in making Banzida a paperless organization. He hated disorder and preferred for everything to be neat and organized.

He looked at the screen and hit send. He heard a buzz and pressed a green button on his desk. The door opened, and two younger men with the bodies of bouncers walked in. He raised his head, stared in their direction, and glared at them.

"Spit it out." His thick voice broke the silence.

The first man said, one of his hands trembling, "We got to Raman. He died in the hospital."

"What about the evidence and the two agents?" Dominic hurled the words at him.

"We have destroyed the evidence. We think the agents are dead. We razed down the hotel they lodged in."

"You think?" Dominic's voice vibrated across the office. "Did you find their bodies?"

"Not yet, sir," the second man replied.

"Find them and kill them."

"Yes, sir," Both men replied in unison.

With a flick of his hand, he dismissed them

The moment the door closed, Dominic banged his fist on the desk, his thick fingers almost breaking it apart.

*****

Three hours later

Twelve men and women sat across a large round table in a windowless room. Dominic Tiza sat in the middle. For five minutes, he spoke in a low tone, and the rest nodded to indicate their agreement. Then he was interrupted by a brown-skinned fortyish man who sat opposite him.

"No, you've changed the plan. This was not what we agreed. This will claim innocent lives."

Glaring at him, Dominic brought a gun from under the table, pointed it at him, and pulled the trigger. The bullet blew off the man's head, scattering pieces of brain matter across the room. The rest of his body fell off the chair.

"Is anyone not on the same page with us?" He stared at their faces—the men and the women.

They all remained quiet. Otherwise, they would follow the path of Ken and others who disagreed with the new plan and wanted to work against them.

Dominic suspected that Raman was having doubts even though he was one of his closest allies. A few days ago, he'd joined Lucas Mordi to terminate Ken. Dominic had gotten reports that Raman was working with Ken. He saw several video footages of them in a meeting. Dominic and Raman were on a team that proposed the new plan. If he was having doubts, it made sense to permanently remove him from the picture. He didn't need to rack his brain over what Raman might do next if he was still alive.

He'd watched the news. The medic believed it was an accident. *Perfect! No loose ends.*

He stared at them. "Mr B talked about innocent lives. Is he serious? Does it equate to the pain and personal loss each of us in this room has suffered in the hands of these criminals?"

"No." The response was uniform, a vote of confidence in his leadership. Now, when he gazed at their faces, he saw the determined resolve in their eyes. His eyes strengthened with resolve.

"Nothing can stop us now. Project Hades is in its final phase. We will launch it straight into the heart of the enemy."

They renewed their oaths to see to the completion of Project Hades. The meeting ended, and everyone in the room departed within an hour. As members of the Banzida board, they were men of means and great wealth who'd sworn to fulfil a common objective.

Dominic watched as the last person, a woman in her early fifties, departed. He pressed a button, and his wheelchair moved towards his private jet. Then, his security men helped and gently carried him into his plane.

He got a message when he settled.

"Target sighted. Should we go ahead?"

He typed, "Yes, terminate," and hit send.

CHAPTER THIRTY-FIVE

A blue taxi stopped in front of an old hotel inside an estate in the Bompai neighbourhood in Kano city. The hotel was two-storey high and had a 1970 architectural design. The vehicle's doors opened. Two people got out—a middle-aged woman with dark sunglasses and an older man in his seventies who carried a huge bag that made him grunt as he walked.

They met the female receptionist in the lobby. There, they booked a room as Mr Bart and Mrs Patricia Adeosun. The brown-skinned receptionist stared at them with pity as she gave the man the key to their room.

She showed them the staircase. The older man grunted as he began to climb. His wife patted him on the shoulder and supported his weight with hers as they took each step. When they got to the first floor, the man took a deep breath, calming down his heart rate before resuming his walk.

At Room 91, the woman collected the key from her husband and opened the door. The moment they entered the room, she locked the door, and both went to sit on the bed.

Ray Okon removed the mask from his face, which made him hot and watched Sarah as she pulled off her wig.

"You are sure no one followed us here?" she asked.

"Yes," Ray said.

Both brought out their pens and notepad.

Ray said, "Banzida. What we know right now is that they are planning to carry out an attack on October Twentieth—the Remembrance Day of Bendi killings."

"Yes. However, we don't know exactly what they are planning, and our only evidence has been destroyed."

"You told me you were decrypting the files before we escaped from the hotel."

She gazed at him. 'Yes, it was at 90% when we left the room. It was so close."

"What can we do right now to delay Banzida from carrying out their attack while we work on stopping them?" Ray asked.

"Kidnap their CEO—the tech billionaire—Dominic Tiza. I think he is a maniac. I saw his picture on the internet. His eyes were red and cold."

Ray thought about it for a moment and then beamed with excitement. "Sarah, how about we tell our supervisors, and they ask the Economic and Financial Crimes Commission to freeze their accounts? They will not have the financial strength to carry out any attack."

Sarah smiled as she stared at him. "Great idea, Ray. Let's do it."

Over the next hour, both agents spoke with their supervisors.

"I think this is unrealistic, Ray," Gideon said to Ray on the phone. He had given him an update about what happened in their former hotel.

Ray talked to him for five minutes, explaining why the plan would work.

"Alright, I will tell my men to draft a letter to EFCC. I will also call the EFCC chairperson to tell him this is urgent."

"Yes, it is, sir."

"We will stop Banzida at all costs," Gideon said.

"We will, sir."

"And Ray."

"Yes, sir."

"These people we are dealing with are a different kind of enemy. Both of you should be careful."

"We will, sir," Ray said, and the call ended.

Sarah had also spoken with her bosses at NIA. "They agreed it is a good plan," she said to Ray when she finished speaking with her boss.

Three hours later, both agents received encrypted messages. Ray opened his phone and read his. "Dear Agent, Banzida Corporation bank accounts have been frozen."

"I got the same message," Sarah said with excitement and embraced him briefly. "We did it, Ray."

"Yes, Sarah. We are close to nailing these criminals."

They remained in a tight hug for a moment longer. When Ray lifted his face and stared at her eyes, he saw how beautiful and spotless her face was. Sparks flew between them. He watched as her lips opened. He tried to fight the emotions welling inside him but couldn't.

He closed his eyes and opened them, and what happened next moved so fast. Sarah crushed her lips on his, and their bodies meshed as they explored each other's mouths. Their kiss deepened as they held each other's waists.

Sarah tugged at his clothes, and Ray didn't know when his two hands had ripped her top and bra apart and held her full ripe breasts. He drove his tongue to her neck and trailed kisses across the soft skin. He heard her let out a sharp moan.

She ripped the buttons off his shirt and began to kiss his chest. Ray brought her lips to his and kissed her hard. She deepened the kiss and tugged her hand on the belt of his trousers. Suddenly, Ray parted his lips away from hers and broke away, breathing hard.

"I'm sorry, Sarah. I am in a relationship."

Sarah's hair was dishevelled. Embarrassment flushed on her face as she stared at him. "Oh, I'm sorry. This shouldn't have happened."

***

In the evening, Ray and Sarah left the hotel dressed in baggy clothes that matched their appearance. They ate dinner in a cool, quiet restaurant close to the estate where their hotel was.

Wherever they went, Ray would scan their surroundings but didn't notice anything out of place. On their way back, he drove through the road illuminated by flashing streetlights and entered a narrow, lonely road. It was another route to the hotel —a necessary security protocol. He didn't want to keep using the same route all the time.

When he slowed down the car to pass over potholes, Sarah, who sat beside him tapped his thigh. "Ray, look ahead!"

Ray saw the headlights and observed as two oncoming vehicles stopped. Five armed thugs spilled out of the cars.

He gripped the steering and frowned "How did Banzida find us?"

Sarah stared back. "I don't know," she said and paused. "There is a car at our back. It's approaching us and moving slowly. I bet it's them."

Ray made a split-second decision. He pressed the gas pedal, the tires screeched, and he took a left and entered the next road ahead of him.

Boom!

Both agents lowered their heads as the back window of their vehicle shattered. Fiery gunfire erupted, destroying the peaceful evening atmosphere in the neighbourhood.

CHAPTER THIRTY-SIX

The car stopped on the right side of the narrow road filled with green grass. Both agents dived out of the car and used it as a shield while dodging bullets. Ray brought out his Beretta and put more bullets in the magazine. When he was going out, he didn't want to take any chances. He knew Banzida would come for them.

He watched as Sarah brought out her Glock and took her position while shielded by the car.

Ray counted the men he'd seen—seven. He dived away from his position as a bullet hit where he was. In the speed of light, he held the gun as he dived, pulling off three shots. He heard grunts as a gunman fell. When he landed on the grass, he watched as Sarah rose. "No," he wanted to say.

"Cover me." Sarah's voice was tight.

Ray kept pulling the trigger as Sarah pulled off multiple shots and ran to the other side of the road, where she merged perfectly with the grass. Three thugs held their stomachs and fell. Another rushed towards Sarah's position. Ray took aim and pulled the trigger. The bullet hit his forehead, and he slumped to the ground.

Ray rose from where he was and ran cautiously along the edge of the road, perching on the sand the moment he reached his destination. Another shooter saw him and raised his gun, but Ray was faster. Three successive bullets hit his chest; he grunted and fell.

His eyes searched for the last gunman. Where was he? He didn't see him. He rose and watched cautiously, his body bent. He entered the road where the assailants parked their cars. He saw the dead bodies and two cars parked on opposite sides of the street.

"Ray!" Sarah's voice came with a sharp warning.

Ray turned but he was too late. A hard kick to his stomach sent him tumbling across the road as his weapon slipped from his hand. He felt a sharp pain in his stomach. He searched for his gun but couldn't find it. He rose and remained on the ground as the shooter approached him.

He was six feet tall and held a knife in his right hand. Ray didn't hear any gunshot from Sarah, so he felt she may have run out of bullets.

The thug rushed over, removed the bullet from his gun and threw the weapon away. "Our boss said we should terminate you. I will cut you open and feed your liver to my crocodile."

He rushed with a knife to where Ray was. Ray dodged him at the last moment while giving him a hard kick in the groin. He grunted. Ray watched as he rose.

The man rushed at Ray. This time, Ray was waiting for him. He sucker-punched the man's face and it sent him reeling on the ground while blood dripped from his mouth. As he tried to rise, Ray watched as a hand grasped the man from the back and wound a rope around his neck; it was Sarah.

The man struggled to kick Sarah and loosen the grip, but she was quick and smart. She applied pressure on his neck with all her strength and tightened the rope around his neck until he laboured to breathe. The man tapped his legs desperately on the ground. He struggled until his strength faded, and his body became still.

Sarah rose, and her gaze met Ray's. They communicated via eye contact and rushed to search the dead attackers. They collected their weapons and searched their pockets but found no IDs. There was nothing to reveal who they were.

"Another dead end," Sarah said.

They went back to their car. As Ray started the engine and drove back to the hotel, he sent a brief update to his boss using his phone. He then called Frank and mouthed quick instructions.

***

Abuja
Loretta parked her back in her office as she prepared to go back home after a busy day. It was six in the evening, and she was exhausted. Her business was growing fast, and she no longer had time for anything else. Five minutes earlier, she had called her best friend, Cynthia.

Cynthia was a nurse who worked in a government hospital. Both had been friends since their university days. Cynthia recently married her heartthrob, Chuks, and was now enjoying marital bliss.

They laughed, and Loretta asked about her husband, Chuks. Cynthia said Chuks was fine and that she was pregnant. Loretta inquired about her health, wished her well, and hung up.

She carried her bag from the desk and left the office. She hit the remote button as she came out of the building, and her Toyota Avensis, a new vehicle she bought a week earlier, beamed with light.

Loretta opened the door and drove the car into the busy Abuja Road two minutes later. As she took the road that would take her to Kubwa, where she lived, she noticed that a vehicle had been trailing her. Her heart raced. To be sure, she entered another road and looked at her side window again. The same vehicle followed her.

Sweat beaded on her forehead, and she gripped the steering wheel tight. When she got close to her house, she stopped. She watched as the vehicle following her stopped, and two men came out and approached her.

Oh my god. What should I do? Panic gripped her.

The men came closer and showed her their badges. She stared at them, her eyes capturing all the details. From what she read, she discovered they were DSS agents.

One of them said, "You have nothing to worry about, ma'am." He gave her a phone. "Someone wants to speak to you."

Is this a trick? What if they were not who they said they were? Her trembling hand collected the phone, and she put it close to her ear.

"Honey, they are our agents. They are now your security detail."

Ray. She heaved a sigh of relief.

Soon, worry spread within her. "What do I need a security detail for? I don't need them."

"Don't worry. They will keep their distance."

Her eyes widened. "Is this about the case? Is there something you are not telling me?"

"Honey, we are just taking precautions. You will be fine."

"Alright, but next time tell me before you make any decision that will affect my life." She reluctantly agreed.

"I love you," Ray said.

"I love you," she replied.

CHAPTER THIRTY-SEVEN

Dominic was in his office checking out a special glass called Esolens 1, a mixed virtual reality device designed by Esiris. They had been working on this project for seven years. Now it was a reality. He was proud of his team. Beside him was a newspaper with the headline—Dominic Tiza and his tech company, Esiris, launches Esolens 1, becoming the first African tech company to join the race to bring Metaverse and Augmented Reality to life. An image of Esolens 1 device was displayed on the front page of the newspaper.

As Dominic picked up the paper to read, he heard a buzzing sound and hit the red button on his desk. The door opened, and a tall, muscular man in baggy jeans entered his office.

"Have you carried out my orders?" he asked.

"I'm sorry, sir." The man trembled. "The two agents killed the men I sent to go after them."

Dominic was filled with rage. He brought out his gun and pulled the trigger. Crimson appeared on the man's stomach, and he fell on the tiled floor. Dominic made a call, and two men in his security detail came with a body bag in less than five minutes and carried the body away.

"Nothing can stop us," Dominic muttered as he relaxed in his seat, but a disturbing image he had of the two agents appeared in his mind. Who were these agents—Ray Okon and Sarah Aderinsola? He brought out his scrambled phone and dialled a number.

"Hello, sir," the voice on the other end said.

"Ray Okon and Sarah Aderinsola. Get me a report on both agents. I want to know everything about them."

"Yes, sir."

He ended the call.

An hour later, he received an email on his laptop. He clicked it open and began to read the document. He got the information that Ray worked in the Department of State Service and Sarah Aderinsola worked in the National Intelligence Agency. It took him twenty minutes to read the whole document. There was nothing vital there. Worse, there was nothing about their families.

He called the number again. "I want more information about them."

"Other information about both agents are classified. We can't access them."

Dominic ended the call and thought about it for a moment. He knew what to do. He pressed a number and waited. The receiver picked on the fourth ring.

"Bruno, I have a job for you."

***

Port Harcourt

Ninety, Ninety-one, Ninety-two... The barrel-chested man whose complexion was the colour of charcoal counted the numbers silently as he worked out in the gym with the free weights. When he reached a hundred, he dropped the weight, grabbed a fitness ball, and began to do crunches. His biceps were precise, and his forearms coursed with veins as they moved up and down.

His phone rang, interrupting him.

He dropped the fitness ball and rose. He wiped the sweat off his face. He wore only white knickers. He picked up his white polo and drank a glass of water. As he gulped down the liquid, sweat dripped over a black scar across his face. When he finished, he went to the table where he kept his phone and picked the call.

He listened as the man on the other end said, 'Bruno, I have a job for you."

He listened as Dominic Tiza spoke for a minute.

"Who?" he asked, curious.

"Ray Okon and Sarah Aderinsola."

He remained quiet.

"Any objection?"

He said, "I know Ray Okon by reputation. Few months ago, he and his team brought down the Dragon Cartel. My fee will triple this time."

"I don't care. Just do it. You will receive the first half of the payment now," Dominic said.

"Okay."

The call ended.

Five minutes later, as Bruno was about to leave the gym, he received a message that told him that the first half of the money had entered his account. The second message read, "Both agents are in Kano."

He put his mobile phone in his bag. He had work to do.

***

At five in the evening, Dominic and five of his men were in a graveyard in a private residence at Makurdi, the capital of Benue, a State in North Central Nigeria. The weather was calm, and the cemetery was deadly quiet. Tears filled Dominic's eyes as he stared at the grave of his beloved sister and brother.

Their parents died when they were young. They used to be the only family he had. Now they were dead; their lives were taken away by the enemy. His brother's grave was unmarked. They never found his body.

He drove his wheelchair closer to where the graves were located, bent and dropped flowers on each of the graves, his expression grim. When he finished placing the second bunch, one of his men brought him his phone. He unlocked it and saw a message.

Bruno: *I am on my way.*

He nodded. This was what he liked about Bruno. He was efficient.

His gaze landed at the two graves for a few more minutes, then he rose. *They will pay*, he said in his mind.

He would hit a dagger at the enemy right in the middle of their hearts.

CHAPTER THIRTY-EIGHT

Ray and Sarah's faces tightened as they watched the large screen in a secure room in a building shared by the Kano State Police Command and the small DSS unit that worked in Kano.

The faces of Ray's boss—Gideon Owolabi, Steve Maccido, and Frank were at three different sections of the screen. The bald head of Sarah's NIA boss, Paul Amaechi, appeared on the fourth section. They were in the middle of an urgent video-conferencing meeting.

Ray scribbled on his notepad. When he raised his head to watch the screen, Gideon was saying, "We suffered a setback. We are facing lawsuits from Banzida."

"What happened, sir?" Ray asked.

Paul raised his head and replied, "The reason is simple. We have no evidence, so the court ordered us to unfreeze their accounts."

Ray saw Sarah slump in her seat. His right hand grazed his temple.

"Agents, here are your orders," Gideon said, "find the evidence. We must stop Banzida."

"They will fail," Frank said.

The meeting lasted for five more minutes before it ended. When they came out of the room,

Ray and Sarah greeted a DSS agent and three police officers and left the building.

They entered the vehicle and took the route to a new hotel at New Road in Sabon Gari, where they lodged.

Sabon Gari was a section of the Kano city reserved for non-indigenes of the State. Ray drove across Sani Abacha way and got caught in traffic when they entered Igbo Road.

They waited under the intense heat of the October sun, their faces filled with sweat. Ray navigated the vehicle to the usually busy France Road when the light turned green. He was surprised when he saw that the road was less busy at this time of the day. He drove fast and slowed down when it was time for him to turn right and enter Court Road.

Suddenly, a huge truck that came from Court Road rammed into them and pushed their vehicle into a nearby gutter. Ray was in a state of shock for the first five seconds and coughed out blood. Out of habit, he stared at Sarah and touched her neck. "Sarah."

Her eyes flew open.

Thank God she is conscious, he thought.

She coughed, and her eyes widened when she realized their car was upside down. Ray did not see the truck, which seemed to have come out of nowhere. His instinct told him something was terribly wrong.

Both agents struggled to climb out of the vehicle. When they finally did, they spat out blood and stared in surprise as five men in black military fatigues surrounded them.

Oh shit, Ray thought.

A six-foot barrel-chested man who carried auto-rifle approached them. "Drop your weapons. Now!"

Sarah brought out her gun and dropped it on the ground.

"Look," Ray said as he brought out his gun and two knives and dropped them on the ground. "We are doing everything you say."

The lead man gazed at one of his men, and he bent and collected their weapons. Suddenly, the lead man brought out another gun from his belt and raised it, pointing it at both agents.

"No. What are you doing? We are not..."

He pulled the trigger and shot Sarah twice in the chest. She grunted in pain and fell.

"Sarah!" Ray screamed.

Two men dragged Ray, put a black cloth around his face, and pulled him hard into the truck. Something hit him hard, and everything turned black.

Ray heard sirens as the vehicle drove off.

CHAPTER THIRTY-NINE

DSS agent Frank Igwe watched Sarah in her hospital room as she lay unconscious on the bed. The attack had shaken the entire agency. No one knew where Ray was taken to. By the time the police got to the scene of the shooting, the gunmen had vanished. A witness who initially refused to talk said the shooters wore black military fatigues. He couldn't recognize their faces.

The police later saw a truck with Abuja license plates parked by the roadside and knew they had changed vehicles. As soon as the police got to the scene of the shooting, they rushed Sarah to the hospital, where the doctor worked for hours to save her life.

Frank had flown from Onitsha to see her as soon as he heard the terrible news. He sat on a metal chair and watched Sarah breathe silently. A drip attached to her arm was connected to the monitor, which showed her heart rate. The first thing he did was to make sure Sarah had adequate security.

The door opened, and a doctor whose nametag read Eugene Nwobodo came into the room. He had a stethoscope around his neck. He walked close to the bed and joined Frank to watch the monitor and observe her. He scribbled notes as he did so.

"She was shot twice. We've removed the bullets. She is a fighter. What saved her life was that she wore a bulletproof vest," Doctor Eugene said.

Relief flooded Frank. He asked the doctor more questions about Sarah, and he answered in his soft-spoken voice.

Frank stayed with Sarah for an hour before leaving the hospital and entered a DSS jet that took him to Lagos.

**

When Frank got to Lagos, a DSS vehicle took him to the DSS Branch office at Ikeja. He realized that the meeting had started when he entered the conference room. His boss—Gideon, Steve Maccido, Inspector James Ibru, Christine Zainab, Sarah's boss at NIA—Paul Amaechi, were seated around the table.

The room was quiet. Sadness covered the faces of all present. They had suffered a huge setback in the case. One of their top operatives had been captured by the enemy. No one knew if he was still alive or if they had shot him dead. The other agent was shot twice. Right now, she was fighting for her life.

"You are late, Frank," Gideon said. "What's the update on Sarah's health?"

Frank apologized for being late and took his time to brief them on Sarah's condition. "The bulletproof vest she wore saved her life. Right now, she is recovering fast and breathing at a normal rate. The doctor said I shouldn't try to wake her up, and I didn't. We are optimistic she will make a quick recovery."

As Frank talked about Sarah, he observed that her boss's face was tight. He knew that Sarah was one of the best agents in her unit. He felt his pain. His fist clenched as he thought of Ray.

"Still no news on Ray..." Steve's voice interrupted his thoughts.

Gideon shook his head.

Paul Amaechi said, "We know how a group like this operates. It's possible they have killed him after extracting information from him—top government secrets that shouldn't be in the wrong hands."

"We never knew Banzida Corporation is behind this," Inspector James said. "I assure all of you that NPF will work with your agencies to rescue Ray and stop the enemy."

Frank's hatred for Banzida grew. "We should arrest Dominic Tiza, the CEO of Banzida."

"We can't arrest him," Gideon said.

"We don't have evidence that connects him and Banzida to the crime," Paul said.

"Now that we've unfrozen their bank accounts, they will move to fasten their plans and carry out the attack," Frank said, frustrated.

Gideon addressed Christine. "Who is the spokesman of Banzida?"

"You mean the man that ranted on social media and claimed that our agencies are attacking Banzida without cause?" Steve said.

Christine typed quickly on her laptop and pulled up an image of a light-skinned man in a Tuxedo. The man's picture appeared on the large screen on the wall.

"His name is Samuel Oviedo. He is the Public Relations Officer of Banzida Corporation. He is known for his expensive dresses and designer wristwatches. He appears on the TV shows, hangs out with celebrities, does photoshoot with politicians during gala parties, and always talks about Banzida in the corporation's YouTube Channel. As the company's spokesman, he is in charge of their branding."

Gideon glanced at Frank. "Set up a meeting with Samuel Oviedo. I heard he talks too much. We may succeed in tricking him into revealing the truth about what Banzida is planning on October twentieth."

Frank nodded.

Gideon turned his attention to Christine. "Find out everything we need to know about Dominic Tiza, including his personal life."

"Yes, sir."

CHAPTER FORTY

Sweat broke across Ray's face as he felt pain all over his body. He was inside a twelve-by-twelve room. The walls were high and painted cream with rough surface. It had only one small window, which was half-open. The stifling heat made it difficult for Ray to breathe.

He didn't know where he was. They had covered his face, brought him there, and closed the door. For days, no one talked to him. There was no noise. Not even from nearby animals. Everything was designed to make the victim go insane. It was as though he was in a maximum-security prison.

His whole body ached. His face itched, and when he attempted to scratch it, a salty droplet of sweat entered his eyes, blinding him with pain. He cried out.

Ray had not eaten much. They only brought water and served him noodles once a day. He was beginning to lose weight. He knew this was a strategy to make him weak so they could easily break him.

At midday, he did push-ups and trained himself to ignore the pain. He'd checked the room and thought of a series of escape plans but discarded each quickly.

He felt a sharp pain in his head, and the painful image of Sarah, when she was shot in the chest, played like a movie behind his eyes. The man had shot her twice. She'd cried out and fell.

"Sarah," he mumbled the word.

They'd killed her. It was obvious.

He clenched his fists and hit them against the wall. Blood covered his hands, and a sharp pain flooded his nerves.

Ray heard a sharp thud, and the door opened. Three men in boots came in, dragged him up, and led him out of the room. They took him to a bigger room, dropped him on a chair, and chained his legs and arms to the seat.

He watched as the man who shot Sarah approached a table close to him, holding a sharp knife. A ball gag, bear trap, cat o' nine tails, hand crushers, hammer, and needle lay on the table.

The man remained standing, his back facing Ray while he continued to test his torture instruments. At that moment, the door opened, and a dark-skinned man in a suit entered the room with a self-driven wheelchair. Ray noticed he had no legs.

His eyes were intense as he flashed Ray a devilish smile. "Oh my God, DSS super-agent, Ray Okon. I've heard so much about you. It's a pleasure to meet you today." There was mockery in his voice.

"Who are you?" Ray asked.

"Oh, I'm sorry for not introducing myself. I am Dominic Tiza. You can call me Dominic."

Ray recognized the name. "The CEO of Banzida Corporation."

The man in the wheelchair grinned. "You've done your research. You got that right." He paused and concentrated on Ray. "You killed my men. Now—"

Ray cut in, "You killed Sarah. You will—"

Ray felt a sharp pain as a blow from the back hit his head, sending stars across his eyes.

"In our culture, when an elderly man is talking, the child is supposed to keep quiet and listen. I hope you have gotten your lesson. Your female agent is dead, disposed like a rag, and left to rot on the roadside. There is nothing you can do about it. Don't waste my time with your childish ramblings, please. We are here to talk about you." Dominic's voice was measured and devoid of emotion.

"No!" The pain about Sarah's death hit Ray in the head like a thud. He struggled until the chain began to cut his skin.

"Here's what we want to know. What does your agency know about Banzida? Give us the information we need, and we will let you go."

"Nothing. We are still in the dark," Ray replied.

"And still, you were able to kill my men. My men sighted you at Nsukka, Ibadan, Kano, and other places where our Leno's Palace branches are located. What were you doing there? Which information are you looking for? Which questions do you want to ask? Hell, you can go ahead and ask me. You and your agency were working with Ken Udeze, isn't that the truth?"

Ray stared at him and remained silent.

"We can do this the hard way or the easy way. Start talking. One last chance."

Ray had enough. "Why are you doing this? Why did you have to kill the university students? What are you planning on October Twentieth?"

When Dominic heard the date, his face tightened. "Enough!"

He stared at the muscle man who assessed the instruments. "Bruno, get me the information I need."

"Yes, boss."

Bruno gave orders, and two men released the chain that bound Ray to the chair. They dragged him to a wooden chair that was close to the table. They chained him to that one, and Bruno plugged a wire attached to the chair to an electric socket. As Dominic left the room in his wheelchair, Ray's painful cries filled the air.

CHAPTER FORTY-ONE

Frank flew back to Abuja the next day and set up a meeting with Banzida PRO, Samuel Oviedo.

At noon, he drove to meet him. Banzida's office building at Abuja Central Business District was majestic and five stories high.

A huge poster was plastered on the wall showing the face of a popular Nigerian musician, Guddo advertising an offer from Ladoo—Banzida Real Estate business.

The company was giving a massive twenty percent discount to its customers and urged them to rush and grab their plots of land before their promo ended.

Frank stared at the wallpaper as he climbed down from his 2016 Toyota Corona while using a remote button to lock the vehicle. He entered the massive building, gave the receptionist his name, and she said, "Take right and enter the elevator to the fourth floor. Samuel, our PRO is patiently waiting for you."

"Waiting for me indeed," Frank muttered under his breath.

Their attempt to present a picture of politeness disgusted him. He did as he was told and took the elevator. It dropped him at the fourth floor. When the door opened, he was surprised to see a man in a blue Tuxedo surrounded by two young women in black corporate suits waiting for him.

The man confirmed the thoughts Frank had in mind.

"Welcome to Banzida Corporation. You must be DSS agent, Frank Igwe."

He nodded.

"I'm Samuel Oviedo, Banzida PRO. The media calls me Banzida Chief Evangelist. Just call me Samuel." He stretched out his hand, and Frank reluctantly brought out his.

Both men shook hands, and he led Frank to his office.

Frank's eyes widened when he saw the office. It was the size of a penthouse suite with white walls and Italian tiled floor. It had two couches, a massive brown desk, and a huge flatscreen that covered the wall. He didn't see bookshelves. There were no papers on the table or in any part of the office.

Samuel showed him the couch, and both men sat. The two ladies left and came back a minute later with a cup of coffee each, which they set on two stools facing the men.

"Coffee, please," Samuel said.

Frank shook his head. "I'm sorry. I'm allergic to it."

"Okay, what drink can we get for you?"

"Don't worry. I don't want to drink anything right now." Frank didn't like his overt politeness. It was clear this was all for show.

This was a corporation that had ordered the killing of innocent people. And they were planning a huge attack in five days. At that moment, a question popped up in his mind. *Where is the evidence?*

He stared at Samuel. Was this chatty fellow Banzida's weak link? Frank was there to find out.

Frank fixed his gaze on Samuel. "We watched a video of you ranting on social media that DSS and the police are harassing Banzida for no reason. You are popular on social media. Your Instagram Page has 1.5 million followers. You are the face of the brand, aren't you? Thousands of your followers said unprintable things about us, casting judgement on an issue they know nothing about, and you couldn't control them. Don't you think you are being overly melodramatic?"

Samuel narrowed his eyes as he stared at Frank. "Am I? When has obeying the law and paying our taxes become a crime? Why did your agency freeze our accounts? Are you working for our competitors? We have nothing to hide. The court knows it, and our clients know it. That's why your case against us fell apart. I'm glad the court did the right thing by ordering you to unfreeze the accounts, which you have done. I simply used social media to raise awareness and show the world and our clients what was going on, and they rushed to our side to support us."

Frank noticed he had an accent. "Did you grow up in Egypt?"

Samuel stared at him for a while, and a warm smile appeared on his face. "Yes. My mother is from

Egypt. I spent the whole of my childhood in Egypt. I only came to Nigeria when I was twenty-one. You should travel to Egypt. Cairo, perhaps. It's a beautiful place with nice beaches, restaurants and—"

"I wish I can. Does Banzida have interest in setting up a branch of Leno's Palace in Cairo?"

Samuel flashed his sparkling white teeth. "It's possible. Let's see what happens."

Frank looked around the office. "I've read a lot about you. You like fine foods, fine wine, and beautiful women. And you love going to parties which you usually attended with Ken Udeze. Both of you look like best friends."

When Frank mentioned the name Ken, colour drained from Samuel's face.

"Ken was killed last week. The police found his body in his room. What happened to Ken? Did Banzida kill him because he knew something he wasn't supposed to know?"

Samuel tightened his fist. "Ken committed suicide. There is no evidence to suggest otherwise. Our corporation has no hand in what happened to him. Is this why you came here to meet me?"

Frank detected anger in Samuel's voice, which confirmed his belief that what Samuel did earlier was all for show. He had shattered his carefully constructed façade.

"Where is Dominic Tiza, the CEO of Banzida?" Frank asked.

"Dominic is not in Nigeria. He is in our headquarters. If you have any information for him, you can give it to me. Be assured that he will get it at the appropriate time," Samuel said sharply.

Frank narrowed his eyes. "I thought this is your headquarters. Where is it located?"

"We moved to Accra in Ghana two years ago. Our followers know this. This is public record. Perhaps you didn't do your research well enough. It's obvious you and your agency have been making wrong assumptions and wild guesses about us."

"Why did you move your headquarters out of the country?"

Samuel flashed him a 'didn't you know already' glance. "Even an idiot knows the answer to your question. Why won't we leave? Nigeria has an unfavourable business environment. You know this already."

Frank could no longer hold his patience. "Your corporation ordered the killing of innocent people. You will pay for it. You will join the rest of your team in spending the rest of your lives in prison, that's if you don't co-operate with us. We can give you immunity if you accept to tell us what we want to know. Where is Banzida keeping Ray Okon? What are you planning on twentieth October?"

Samuel rose quickly from his seat, a deep frown on his face. "Enough. We are done here. This is unbelievable. We will sue you to court for accusing us of murder." He pointed at the door. "Please leave my office. If you have evidence against us, bring it forward. Otherwise, you are wasting my time."

Frank fumed in anger. He stared at Samuel and stormed out of the office.

When he left the building and got into his car, he got a call from Loretta and picked it.

"Frank, where is Ray? I have not heard from him for days." Her voice was trembling.

He took a deep breath and spoke calmly. "Ray went to a special ops mission. I'm not allowed to share the details with you. He is not allowed to use his mobile phone during the mission. Don't worry about it; he will be back soon."

"Don't bullshit me, Frank. I can detect when you are lying to me. Something has happened to him." She began to sob.

Frank tried to calm her.

When he ended the call, he sent a brief encrypted message to his boss using their channel.

As he drove through the busy Abuja roads, he made plans to take a flight back to Kano and meet with Sarah.

CHAPTER FORTY-TWO

A lethal whip struck Ray's back, and he cried out in pain. He was in the room Bruno called Hall of Pain. Six hours after he'd passed out on the electric chair, two men had unchained him, dragged him up, and chained his hands to two metal plugs in the wall. His legs were chained to a metal attached to the ground.

Ray hung there with his arms and legs stretched while Bruno asked him questions and struck his back with the lethal whip.

The pain was blinding him.

"We know the truth," Bruno said as he walked closer to him. "We saw everything in the video footage. We saw that agent your agency planted in Leno's palace, UNN. She worked for six months as a waitress, right? In the video footage, she was in a meeting with Ken, and the coward was talking to her. The only problem is that the video was messed up, and we couldn't hear their voices. I want to ask you just one question. Tell me, and your pain will end. What did Ken tell your agent during that meeting?"

Ray responded by spitting at Bruno's face.

The spit hit him as he opened his mouth to talk.

"You rat!" he bawled and stared at the two men beside him.

They held Ray's body in the perfect position. Bruno raised the whip and slammed it hard against Ray's wounded skin on his back. The pain hit Ray hard, making his entire body tremble.

"We've killed your female agent like a coward that she was. We will kill you too if you don't start talking. You made a deal with Ken, didn't you? After that meeting, he knew he had bitten the hand that fed him. He pasted that list in his room before he died, just like an amateur that he was." Bruno laughed.

"It is obvious you killed him," Ray said.

Bruno glared at Ray and said between gritted teeth, "No one can stop Banzida. No one can stop the project."

Ray heard him and dropped his gaze to him. "Which project?"

"Shut up! You are not in charge here. I am." Bruno lashed out like an angry dog. "Tell me everything your agency knows about Banzida. What did Ken tell you? You have caused the death of three of our branch managers. Our last question, what did Lucas Mordi tell you before he died?"

Ray stared at him for a moment, the pain hitting his nerves. "You will fail. Banzida will fail. Right now, our agency is tracking me. They are coming for you. They would soon be here and raze everything to the ground. You will pay for your crimes."

"Shut up!" Bruno shouted, and his rage took over. He let it loose on Ray's body, hitting his back with the whip without control.

Ray cried out.

Bruno continued to unleash his rage on him.

Two minutes later, Ray's world went dark.

CHAPTER FORTY-THREE

Frank flew back to Kano and arrived in the evening. He lodged in a hotel and took a cab to the hospital where Sarah was being cared for. It was the sixteenth of October, four days to twentieth.

The tension in the agency was high. No one knew what Banzida was planning nor how to stop them. Worse, Ray Okon, their lead agent, was missing. All their efforts to track him had failed. Frank cringed at the thought of what might have happened to him. From what he'd observed, Banzida was ruthless and had always been ten steps ahead.

He hoped Sarah would be awake. The information she had would be critical in stopping the enemy. He also hoped she would still remember what happened before she was shot.

Frank beamed when he entered Sarah's ward and saw she was conscious. She was eating fried potato while watching the NTA breakfast show on the TV, which hung on the wall across from her bed.

A warm smile appeared on her face when she looked up and saw him. "Frank, you came."

Relief flooded Frank. He took her reaction as a good sign that her memory was still intact. He placed the bread and apple juice he bought for her on the table. She tried to shift her position and winced in pain.

Frank raised his hand and said, "No, remain as you are. Don't stress yourself, please."

She nodded, looked at him with her probing eyes, and said, "Oh, Ray." Tears filled her eyes, "Where is Ray? They took him, isn't it?"

Frank noticed what was happening and intervened, "No, Ray is fine."

It was too late. The monitor began to beep, and two nurses rushed into the ward. "Her temperature is up. Call the doctor!" the older nurse said to the younger one.

She rushed to call the doctor. The elderly nurse glared at Frank with anger in her eyes. "She was fine until you came here. What did you do?"

The doctor rushed in. They worked for thirty minutes and stabilized her. Frank apologized to her medical team and explained who he was.

"Sarah is fine now. Give her some time to rest. You can stay here but be quiet. Don't talk to her for now. You can talk to her in the evening," Dr Eugene said.

Frank thanked the doctor. Sarah's medical team left a minute later. He remained in his seat and watched Sarah as she slept, observing the rise and fall of her chest. So many things were on his mind. They were losing time, but Sarah's health was his priority. He stayed with her till evening.

"You are still here." Her voice made him wake up.

He opened his eyes and wiped the sleep from his eyes. He asked her how she was feeling, and for the next twenty minutes, they chatted and had light conversations about the kindness of the nurses and the calmness of the weather.

Then out of the blues, she asked, "Where is Ray?" This time, her voice was stable.

Frank fixed his gaze on her and said, "We don't know yet. We assume he is still alive. We are doing everything possible to locate and rescue him. What do you remember about the attack?"

Sarah closed her eyes for a moment. When she opened them, she said, "I saw a huge dark-skinned man with four other men. It was clear he was their leader. He talked and gave the orders. They held Ray after they surrounded us and asked us to drop our weapons. The man pointed his gun at me. I remember falling. I can't remember anything else."

Frank kept asking probing questions, ensuring Sarah was stable and calm.

Ten minutes later, Sarah requested a pencil and a sheet of paper.

Frank watched her in surprise as she began to draw in silence. He knew the conversation had ended.

CHAPTER FORTY-FOUR

Frank took the sketch from Sarah and flew back to Lagos the following day. Two hours later, he received a message that they had an important meeting.

A light rain was falling in Lagos when Frank arrived. As he entered the vehicle that took him to the venue of the meeting, he observed pedestrians rushing to go to their destinations, and it reminded him of how important their job as law enforcement agents was.

As security and law enforcement agents, they worked behind the scenes to fight crime and preserve law and order. Sometimes, to succeed, they had to put their lives on the line.

Frank's driver took him to Victoria Island and dropped him inside a secured white bungalow patrolled by police and four soldiers. Their bosses decided to choose a more secure location because of the sensitive nature of the meeting.

He entered the building and headed straight to the conference room. He met his boss, Gideon, Steve Maccido, Christine Zainab, and police representative Inspector James Ibru. He stared at their sad faces as he took his seat. It was as though he could read their thoughts.

The time was 10:00 am on October seventeenth. Their lead agent, Ray Okon, was still nowhere to be found. Right now, no one knew what Banzida was planning nor if there was any connection between Banzida and the victims of the university students' case.

Frank felt someone tap his shoulder. "The sketch, please."

He looked up. It was Christine.

"Oh, yes." He pulled out a large envelope from his briefcase, opened it, removed the sketch, and gave it to her.

Everyone watched as she put it in a scanner that sat close to high-tech hardware in the room. When she finished scanning the document, a picture of a huge, tall man pointing a gun at a young woman appeared on a large screen which hung on the wall.

Christine ran the picture on DSS facial recognition software. It revealed the face of a dark-skinned man along with his details. Christine worked with a laptop projected to the screen. "His name is Bruno Tema. He is a former soldier who worked in the Nigerian Army. He was dismissed dishonourably from the military in 2005 for insubordination." Christine spoke as her fast fingers hit the keyboard. "Since then, no one heard anything about him. However, a quick search on the dark web showed he is a contract killer who works for the highest bidders."

"So, he went rogue after being dismissed from the military. We are getting close," Gideon said. He turned to James Ibru, "James, we'd like the police to put his picture on the news and put a 20-million-naira price tag on his head."

"So that anyone with information about his whereabouts should contact us," James added.

"Yes," Gideon said.

"We still don't know the connection between Banzida and the University Students' case, nor if Ray is still alive or dead," Frank said.

Silence enveloped the conference room.

Gideon broke the silence and said, "Let's get to work. If we find Bruno, we will stop Banzida."

CHAPTER FORTY-FIVE

At 4:30 pm, Gideon Owolabi stepped out of his government-owned Sienna vehicle he used in Abuja. Two DSS agents surrounded him. He glanced around the marbled compound before he fixed his gaze at the brick building in front of it. It was a secure DSS CID Safe House where they were keeping Sarah.

Two hours earlier, Frank had briefed him that she had been discharged from the hospital in Kano and transferred to the DSS CID Safe House in Abuja. Gideon then flew to Abuja to meet them.

An agent opened the door for him and his men when they approached the entrance. They passed along a vast hallway and took a right. Gideon looked ahead and saw Frank approaching him when they reached a bend.

"Welcome, sir," Frank greeted. Frank had travelled back to Abuja immediately after the meeting.

"How is she doing?"

"She is recovering fast and just left the gym where she did a mild exercise."

Gideon frowned. "Isn't that too early?"

"She was adamant. I had no option but to give in."

"Where is her room?"

"This way, sir," Frank said and led the way.

They followed him as he turned right and entered the last room in the hallway. As Gideon and his men approached, the muscle agents guarding the room greeted him. He flashed them a smile and returned the greeting.

"Wait here," Gideon said to the men who came with him.

"Yes, sir," they said in unison.

Gideon opened the door, entered the room along with Frank, and closed the door behind him. Sarah sat in an armchair watching the news.

A female correspondent was reporting about the university students' case. "Their deaths sent shockwaves across the country. The people we interviewed on the streets said the answer given by the police and the DSS are not good enough. Till now, no one knew why these final year students from different universities had to take their own lives. We—"

Sarah pushed a button on the remote and muted the news. She looked in Gideon's direction and attempted to stand.

"No, please. Remain on your seat," Gideon cut in and rushed to her side. "Have you heard from your superiors?" Gideon asked.

"Yes, I spoke with my boss, Paul Amaechi this afternoon. He will come to see me tomorrow."

"Great. Sarah, thank you for your bravery. With your help, we've gotten the identity of the man who led the attack against you and Ray," Gideon said.

"His name is Bruno Tema," Frank said. He went on to explain to her who he was.

"Any news on Bruno since then?" Sarah asked. "What about Ray?"

"None so far, but we are working on it," Frank said.

"We don't have time. Today is seventeenth," Sarah said, her voice revealing her frustration.

Gideon sank on a chair. He was tired and worried. His bosses were pressuring him to get his acts in order and solve the case after a crime reporter who reported on the case called the handling of the university students' case by Nigerian Law Enforcement Agencies a national disaster. If he didn't get the situation under control soon, they might axe him, and all the sweat and years he had put into his work as a DSS officer in the service of his country would be in vain.

No, he would not let this happen.

"But, wait." Frank's voice made him snap out of his deep thoughts. "If Banzida is behind this, how did they kill the students? We are presuming the students didn't commit suicide."

"It's possible they monitored them for months and finally found a weak link which they used to their advantage to kill them," Sarah said.

"How?" Frank asked.

Sarah opened her mouth to answer, but Gideon cut in, "It's alright, Sarah. Rest for now. We will stop Banzida."

"I will never forgive myself if anything bad happens to Ray," Sarah said as tears filled her eyes.

Ray Okon, Gideon thought as he clenched his fist. *Where are you? What have they done to you?*

CHAPTER FORTY-SIX

Ray opened his eyes. He instantly closed his lids as a bright light hit them. Then, he heard voices.

"He is awake. But you need to be careful."

"Doctor, just do your job. Call me when you are through."

Two seconds later, he heard a door open then close.

He opened his eyes again and winced in pain.

The man beside him touched his leg. "Sorry."

"Sorry?" Ray's blood boiled.

He glanced around the room and observed that they had moved him from where he was. He was in a tiny room, and a man in a white lab coat was attending to his leg. He remembered that someone had called the man 'Doctor.' Suddenly, a sharp pain shot through him as the medic began to sew a part of his badly wounded right leg. When he finished, he wrapped a bandage around it.

Ray observed that the chain on his leg had been removed so the doctor could work on it. He became alert when the doctor finished checking the various parts of his battered body. He rubbed a pain relief cream on his Ray's body, and Ray cried out as the pain flooded him.

"Sorry."

Ray became quiet as his mind worked on an idea. He knew what would happen next, but his hands were still chained to the metal beside him.

"Bisha." The doctor called out.

A voice from inside the room said, "Have you finished, doc?"

"Yes."

"Don't die yet," the doctor said and left the room.

Bisha approached Ray.

Ray's eyes focused on the phone he was pressing. He assumed he was chatting with his someone. Another man came forward, a second guard. Both muscle men were in their twenties or early thirties. Both carried rifles. Ray knew he needed to act fast. It was now or never.

As Bisha came closer to gaze at his face, Ray swung his legs and scissored Bisha's neck. The pain shot through his body, but he tightened his legs on Bisha's neck. Rattled, the second guard lifted his gun and aimed. Ray quickly used Bisha as a shield, and the bullet hit Bisha. Furious, the guard pulled the trigger again, but in a split second, Ray dived out of his bed and used all his strength to pull on the chain in his hands. The rusted metal it was attached to came off, and as the second guard attempted to pull the trigger, Ray hit his head with the metal and gripped his neck with his hands.

At that moment, the door opened, and two more guards stepped in. Ray used the second guard as a shield as the burst of gunfire started. The guard gave up the ghost as the bullets battered his body. Ray collected a pistol from the dead man's belt and quickly pulled the trigger killing the two guards. He shifted from his position as the body of the second guy fell on the floor. He collected an auto rifle from the dead guard and moved close to the door.

He heard voices and approaching footsteps. Three shooters entered through the door, and he mowed them down with bullets. He knew it was dangerous to remain in the room. He needed to move out before they alerted Bruno to come back with more men if they hadn't already.

Ray collected the key from the pocket of the first guard, unlocked the chain on his hand, and limped out the room. A guard appeared at the end of the other hallway, and Ray pulled the trigger. The guard fell dead on the floor.

As he moved, his wounded body slowed him and he almost wanted to shut down, but he forced himself to stay awake and remain focused. He took a left and pulled the trigger repeatedly, killing three more guards.

He moved faster. But as he turned left to enter a dark alley, a knife slashed close to his body. He dodged it at the last minute and turned to see a guard with a sharp knife. The angry guard hurled himself at Ray still holding the knife.

Ray moved left while hitting him hard in the groin. The knife fell, and his legs buckled. Ray collected the knife and slammed it hard into his stomach.

"You can't stop the project," The guard managed to say as blood poured from his mouth.

"What?"

Ray stared at his face and saw that his eyes were open, and he'd stopped breathing. He looked up and saw a fence at the end of the dark alley. He ran towards it and climbed it. He landed on a narrow road filled with grass.

The alarm blared, and he heard Bruno's voice shouting orders.

Ray ran across the narrow road, his bullets hitting two gunmen who came out from the building. He kept running until he hit a dead-end. *No!* His mouth hung open.

He heard approaching footsteps at his back. He stood where the path ended. He looked toward the edge and saw a river that lay far below.

Bursts of gunfire shattered the few seconds of silence. A bullet missed him as he reached the edge. There was no other option. He glanced back and saw Bruno and five armed thugs running towards him. A bullet hit him as he turned.

He jumped. His legs lifted in the air, and his body fell until it hit the river below.

CHAPTER FORTY-SEVEN

Arnold, a dark-skinned twelve-year-old boy, came out from a mud house and ran to a kiosk across the road. It was ten on Sunday morning, and his father had given him a list of things to buy.

"What do you want, Arnold?" the shop owner asked him as soon as he entered the store.

The boy gave him the list. The shop owner, a middle-aged woman with a wrinkled face, perused the handwritten note on the crumpled white paper and began bringing out the items on the list. When she was done, she put them in a plastic bag and gave them to the boy.

"*Oya*, give this to your father. Tell him I added extra," she said in Nigerian Pidgin English.

Arnold thanked her and left. He looked right and left before crossing the road. Next to him was a signboard of Christ Church Redeemers Parish, Auchi. He rushed into the compound, entered their mud house, and gave his father the plastic bag.

His father brushing his tobacco-stained teeth, looked at him and asked, "Is everything here?"

"Yes, Papa. She added extra."

His father smiled. "Mama Ejima." He glanced at his son. "Check to see if the visitor is awake."

The boy nodded, left his father's room, and entered the tiny corridor. He walked to the last room on the right and opened the door. He watched with excitement as the visitor's eyes with a bandaged body, opened.

***

Ray opened his eyes and saw a young boy. Their eyes met, and the boy said, "Father, he is awake."

Confusion filled Ray. He looked around the room. He was in a different place. Memories of what happened hours ago came rushing back, and he felt the stab of pain in his chest. *Bruno. The gunmen. The river.*

"Thank God you made it."

Ray followed the direction of the voice and saw a dark-skinned man who appeared to be in his sixties. A stick was wedged between his teeth.

"What do you remember?"

Ray shut his eyes and opened them. He tried to sit, but the pain hit him hard.

"Take it easy."

"I was in a river. How did I get here?"

The man nodded. "Either the river washed your body close to the shore, or you swam till you reached the shore. A fisherman saw your body early in the morning and called us. We brought you out and pumped lots of water out of your body until you cried out. That was when we knew you were alive. I'm the landlord of this building. We brought you here. Since then, my wife has been taking care of you. We removed a bullet from your shoulder.

She applied herbs on your skin. Your wounds will heal," the man explained.

"Where is she?"

"She went to the market to buy foodstuff."

"Thank you for saving my life."

The man smiled. "You are lucky. Don't thank me, thank God."

"Please, I need a phone."

"Alright," the man said.

He left the room and returned with a mobile phone. He handed it to Ray.

"Thank you," Ray said as he collected the phone. He pressed the numbers he knew by heart.

"Please, enter your code," a female voice said in his ear.

Ray mentioned his code.

"Location, please."

"Where am I?" he asked the man.

"Auchi in Edo state."

A DSS private jet picked up Ray an hour later and flew him back to Abuja. The pilot landed in Nnamdi Azikiwe International Airport, and a vehicle took him to the DSS CID secret safe house at Wuse, the same place where Sarah was staying.

CHAPTER FORTY-EIGHT

DSS CID Safe House, Wuse, Abuja.
Smiling faces met Ray upon entering the safe house. Frank, Steve, Sarah, Christine, Gideon, and the rest of the members of the DSS CID were there. Each hugged him.

"Welcome back, agent Ray. We are glad you are alive," Gideon said as he hugged him and patted him on the back. Ray cringed in pain but covered it up with a smile.

"Welcome back, Ray. I'm glad you are here," Frank said and gave him a tight hug.

"Oh, Ray." Sarah rushed to his side, hugged him, and refused to let go. "I thought I wouldn't see you again."

The moment was emotional for them. The memories of what they went through flashed in Ray's mind.

After greeting each person in the house, he was given a room where he brushed, showered, and wore a new set of clothes. His body was still battered, but his wounds were starting to heal.

For an hour after he got dressed, he remained silent in the room, gathering his thoughts. He'd checked the date and found out it was the nineteenth day of October. He stared at the clock on the wall. It was 5 pm. Time was running out. He didn't want to think of the consequences if they failed to stop the enemy.

Someone knocked on the door. Ray opened it, and the agency's shrink, Dr Andrew Bayo, entered.

They greeted, and for the next two hours, Ray went through the debriefing process, a standard procedure in the agency used to find out information a previously captured agent shared with the enemy.

Andrew asked pointed and sensitive questions that forced Ray to relive the horrors of his stay in the hands of Bruno and his men. When they finished, Dr Andrew scribbled on his notepad and left.

Exhausted, Ray fell into a deep sleep. He woke up at 6:30 the following morning, brushed, showered, and dressed. After eating, he received a text message from the team. They had an emergency meeting. His eyes widened when he discovered it was the twentieth of October, and they still had no idea how to stop the enemy.

Ten minutes later, Ray left his room, walked across the hallway, and entered the conference room.

Gideon, Sarah, Christine, Zainab, Steve, and the rest his team members sat at the rectangular table. Gideon started by asking Ray to tell them everything he observed while in the hands of the enemy.

Ray began to speak and talked for eight minutes, telling them everything he knew.

"Wait," Gideon cut in.

"You said one of their men talked about a project?"

Ray glanced in Gideon's direction. "Yes, he said we can't stop the project. I asked him what he meant but later discovered he had given up the ghost."

There was silence in the room. Only Christine Zainab was busy hitting the keyboard of her PC. Her screen was projected to the big screen in the room.

"I also met Dominic Tiza." Ray dropped it like a bombshell, and all eyes stared at him.

"He came?" Steve asked.

"Yes."

"This means we are correct. Banzida is behind these attacks," Sarah said.

"He mocked us and said we are going to fail," Ray said and watched the big screen where Christine Zainab typed Dominic Tiza's name on Google. She dragged the cursor to scroll to the next page.

"Christine, wait." Ray cut in.

She stared at him. "What is that?"

"Click on the third result."

Christine shifted her gaze to the screen. "You mean an article about Dominic Tiza donating to a non-governmental organization. He does this every time. He is also a philanthropist. We've searched his record. There is nothing there." The frustration in her voice was distinct.

"Open it, please," Ray said.

She clicked the article, and the page opened. "Business Mogul and Tech Giant, Dominic Tiza, donates 5 million dollars to Justice For Miriam Foundation," she read the title.

"Keep reading. Continue to scroll down," Ray said.

Everyone's eyes were on the screen.

"President of the organization, Stella Odi, thanked Dominic for his generosity and said they would carry out his request. She said the money would be used to build a statue in honour of Miriam Tersoo."

"Who is Miriam Tersoo?" Ray asked.

Christine scrolled down and stopped. "Miriam Tersoo was a twenty-year-old young girl who was killed in 2011 by Tactical Anti-Crime Squad, TACS. The incident sent shockwaves across the country and raised people's outrage against the government. Her death was captured on video, and it made news headline for three months," Christine said and kept tapping the keyboard. "TACS—Tactical Anti-Crime Squad—was a tactical police unit accused of brutality, extortion, and extrajudicial killing. Their victims were the young people in the country. The youths raised outrage against TACS during the EndTACS protest, and government yielded to their demand and banned the police unit during the nationwide protest," Christine read.

TACS. EndTACS Protest. The two words hit Ray hard. His gut told him both words held the answer to unravelling the plot Banzida was planning. "Go on, Christine," Ray said.

"Stella Odi founded the Justice For Miriam Foundation in 2012 after Miriam's death and used the organization to rally people together and fight for her justice. Over the years, Justice For Miriam Foundation has grown to become a powerful non-governmental organization that fights against injustice and promote women empowerment. They were also prominent during the EndTACS protest of 2018."

"What about her family? What do we know of Miriam's siblings?" Frank asked.

Christine answered while staring at the screen, "Miriam had two brothers. Their parents died when they were kids and the eldest, Dominic Tersoo began to take care of the younger ones. The name of the other brother is Patrick Tersoo. The first time we heard about the family was in 2003 when Dominic Tersoo emerged as the winner of International Tech-Hub For Young Mobile App Developers Event which held at Silicon Valley in United States.

"Dominic had built an App which would help National Agency for Food and Drugs Administration and Control (NAFDAC) to detect fake drugs. For winning the prize, Dominic was awarded 1-million-dollar grant and got scholarship to study AI and Computer Engineering at Massachusetts Institute of Technology—MIT in United States. The next time the family appeared on the news was in 2011 when Miriam Tersoo was killed by a member of TACS. There is no information about the brothers. There are reports that Patrick Tersoo was among the people killed during the Bendi Massacre which took place during the EndTACS protest but no one could verify the information. No one knows if the two brothers are still alive."

"Wait a minute," Gideon cut in. "I want to find out everything we know about Dominic Tersoo."

Everyone became alert. They all watched as the image of a dark-skinned young man in his early twenties appeared on the screen.

"This is Dominic Tersoo. This was the only picture I could find. Here, he was twenty-four years old. I think he took this picture in 2011," Christine said.

"2011, the year his sister Miriam was killed," Ray said. "Get Dominic Tiza's picture and put both on our Facial Recognition Software.

Christine brought out a recent picture of Dominic Tiza. He had different facial features. He was dark-skinned, looked sharp, and wore a tuxedo.

Christine ran both pictures on the Facial Recognition Software, and everyone gasped as they watched the screen. "99.9% percent match," Christine said as she read the result.

"This was why we didn't know any personal information about Dominic Tiza. He is Dominic Tersoo. He changed his name to Dominic Tiza and scrubbed his past from the record books," Ray said.

CHAPTER FORTY-NINE

Silence fell in the room as everyone took in the information.

"Christine, you said there are reports that Patrick Tersoo was killed during the EndTACS protest," Ray said.

"Yes, unverified reports. The reports said he was shot dead on the day of the Bendi Massacre."

"What's today's date again?" Ray asked.

"Twentieth October 2018."

An idea hit Ray. "Oh my God. Dominic is crippled."

"Yes, it is a public knowledge," Steve said.

"The question is—what made him to be crippled? In the old picture, Dominic had both legs. I think Dominic joined his brother during the protest. His brother got killed, and he was wounded."

"Hmmm," Sarah muttered.

"And today is the anniversary of the Bendi killing," Frank said.

"Is there any special event in connection to the EndTACS protest that is happening today?" Ray asked.

"Let me check," Christine began to type.

Gideon said, "Yes, members of EndTACS Panel of Inquiry will be presenting a book to the members of Federal Executive Council and top dignitaries during the event. Our agency got the memo."

"Where is the event holding?" Frank asked.

"Royal Pyramid Hotel, Abuja. The book contains their recommendations, including the way forward for the country," Gideon replied.

"I just found something!" Christine shouted.

"What?" Ray, Frank, and Steve asked in unison.

"Our chief mentioned EndTACS Panel of Inquiry."

"And?" Ray said.

"I just found what the victims of the University Students' case have in common. I guess this is the reason Banzida killed them," Christine said.

**

"What do they have in common?" Ray asked.

"See for yourself," Christine said, and everyone stared intently at the screen.

Christine had opened a page that showed the names of members of EndTACS Panel of Inquiry.

"Senator Vincent Magu, Chairman of EndTACS Panel of Inquiry," Frank read. "He is the father of…"

"Destiny Magu, one of the victims," Ray chipped in.

"Next on the list is the Honourable Badmus Onyeama," Christine said.

"He is the father of Nonso Onyeama, one of the victims," Steve said with a frown.

Ray stared at the screen. "Next is Senator David Adebayo. Isn't he the uncle of Ifeoluwa Oladipo? She is one of the victims. Oh my God!"

"Next is Stephen Abada, former Inspector General of Police," Gideon said.

"He is the father of Gaius Abada, one of the victims," Sarah said.

"Oh my God!" Steve muttered.

Christine removed her eyes from the screen and stared at their faces. "Banzida was killing the children of the members of EndTACS Panel of Inquiry."

"Dominic is hurt. He lost his twin brother during the protest. His sister was killed by TACS. This looks like a well-orchestrated payback," Frank said.

"The panel was set up to investigate activities of TACS. There were reports that young people were killed during the EndTACS protest, especially during the infamous Bendi massacre. The youths accused Government officials of sending law enforcement agents to shoot at them during the protest. Those agents allegedly killed some of the protesters at Bendi Tollgate during the protest on the night of October 20th. The government set up the panel to investigate all the cases and make sure that justice is served. But there are reports that members of the panel collected bribes and declared they found no evidence that government or law enforcement agencies were at fault," Christine explained.

"The whole EndTACS issue is a sensitive one. There is no evidence yet. However, the members of the panel denied collecting bribes," Steve said.

"Dominic and his colleagues are probably heaping the blame on members of the panel. They started by targeting their children. Since then, they have been operating under the radar. Now, it's obvious they want to kill them all, including the innocent people who will be at the event," Ray said.

"Who else will be at the event?" Frank asked.

"The president and members of the Federal Executive Council, top politicians in the country, selected members of the media and members of the civil society organizations," Gideon replied.

As Ray removed his eyes from the screen, he remembered something he heard from Bruno while he was in the dungeon. Bruno was making a phone call at the time. He was close to Ray. Ray assumed Bruno thought he was sleeping. Five hours earlier, they had given him an injection that put him to sleep after torturing him and seeking information he refused to provide. But Ray was awake then and heard Bruno mention a name while on the phone. Ray had forgotten it, but when the memory of what happened at that time rose to the surface of his mind, he remembered it. "Project Hades."

"What?" Sarah asked.

Ray looked at them. "Banzida wants to wipe them out—everyone that would be in that building during the event. The ultimate payback.'

"When will the event begin?" Sarah asked.

Christine said, "Now, it's 8:00 am. The event will begin by 10 am."

The tension in the room rose to its limit.

Gideon glanced at them and said, "If this plan goes ahead, it will tear the country apart. Stop Project Hades at all cost and arrest Dominic and his cohorts."

CHAPTER FIFTY

Dominic Tiza drove across the main corridor of his luxuriously lavished residence with his wheelchair and headed to his study. When he entered the room, he fixed his gaze at the two big portraits on the wall. They were pictures of his brother, Patrick, and his sister, Miriam. Both were dead, killed by their enemy.

Their parents died in a ghastly motor accident when they were kids. As the first child, Dominic took the responsibility of raising his siblings. Abandoned by uncles and family members from both their maternal and paternal families, they suffered over the years of their childhood and hawked foodstuff just to survive.

What saved the kids from starvation was Dominic's special gift. He was brilliant, especially in Mathematics and science. Their parents had died when Dominic had just finished his primary school education. With faith, he hawked foodstuffs and used the money to buy examination forms to take entrance examination in a government school at Yaba Technical College, Lagos.

At that time, he didn't know how he would pay his school fees. However, he got the highest score among all the students who took the examination. He scored 100% and didn't lose any marks. It was a feat no one had achieved before in that school.

Delighted, the school authorities offered him a scholarship which included a monthly allowance. Dominic sent part of the allowance to his siblings. That was how he survived at school. He loved mathematics and sciences but was curious about computers and spent a lot of time in the school's computer room, learning how to code.

When his form teacher, who was also his computer teacher, discovered the young man's special interest in the subject, he encouraged him. Dominic graduated top of his class from secondary school at the age of sixteen. His form teacher approached him the next day, his face filled with delight. He told Dominic about an international coding and mobile app development competition for teenagers and asked him to apply. Before he applied, Dominic had already founded his company—Esiris—in his bedroom. It was his idea of a tech company.

After his teacher's visit, Dominic began developing an app which was the main requirement for those participating in the competition.

Three months later, Dominic won a one million dollars grant when he emerged as the winner of the International Tech-Hub For Young Mobile App Developers Event held in Silicon Valley, California, in the United States. In the competition, Dominic built a mobile app to help National Agency for Food and Drug Administration and Control (NAFDAC) detect fake drugs.

Subsequently, he was given a scholarship to study AI and Computer Engineering at Massachusetts Institute of Technology in the United States. Four years later, he emerged as one of the top graduates of his class. He applied for a grant to fund his rebranded start-up tech company, Esiris, and won it six months later.

Since then, he'd scaled his business, expanded his operations, and generated profit in the process.

Three years ago, he'd teamed up with other partners to acquire Banzida Corporation. Today, he was Africa's youngest billionaire. But that was far from his thought right now.

His gaze shifted from his brother's photograph and settled on his sister's huge portrait. The girl in the picture was a spectacular ebony beauty with a pointed nose, brilliant eyes, and dimples on her cheeks. He'd gotten the portrait for her on her twentieth birthday, the year she was killed.

CHAPTER FIFTY-ONE

Dominic Tiza clenched his fist as he stared at the portrait of his late sister, Miriam. She was full of life. She had a stubborn streak but was always energetic and knew what she wanted. They were so close. When Dominic was in the United States, he communicated with her more than he did with Patrick. She was his beloved sister.

He brought out a smartphone from his pocket and placed his thumb on the screen. The phone unlocked the moment it captured his fingerprint. He went to his video player, saw the video he wanted, and clicked play.

"Officer, why are you harassing us? I didn't do anything wrong," a female voice shouted in the video.

"Oh my God. Officer, we didn't do anything wrong," another female voice pleaded.

"I said come out of the car right now!"

Dominic watched as the officer who made the statement brought out his gun.

At that moment, the passenger door opened, and a girl with a pink top and jeans alighted quickly from the car. "Jesus, he is with a gun! Miriam, just do what he said."

"Why should I do that?" the girl inside the car replied to her friend. "He asked for my driver's licence and papers, and I showed him. He saw that everything is in order. Why is he asking me if I am the owner of the car?" She stared at the TACS official. "I've told you already. I'm the owner of the car. Today is my birthday. My elder brother bought this car for me. I recently graduated from the University. I am just coming back from campus with my friend, Lilian when you stopped us. I didn't break any law. Why are you harassing us?"

"I don't believe you. On the count of three, drop the key in the ignition and come out of that car," the officer ordered.

Dominic's face tightened as he watched the video. He could feel the tension as he watched the scene unfold. He saw five people observing what was going on with fear in their eyes. The direction of the camera shifted. He heard a noise and then the sound of a gun.

Thaw. Thaw. Thaw.

"Oh my God. He shot Miriam. He just shot Miriam." Her friend, Lilian, began to cry.

Dominic's hands trembled. He watched as people surrounded the new vehicle he bought for his beloved sister as her birthday gift. Tears filled his eyes when he saw the blood that splashed at the driver's door.

Five seconds later, he heard a vehicle leaving.

"He shot her and ran away with his car. He is a TACS official. He just ran away." The voice making the announcement broke into a sob.

"We need help here. Miriam. Miriam!" Lilian cried out.

"Miriam has stopped breathing," another voice said.

Dominic paused the video and dropped the smartphone on the chair beside him. He couldn't control his emotions any longer. He remembered how he felt when he first watched this video in 2011, three days after his sister's tragic death. Helpless. He sank in his chair as another uncontrollable sob tore from his throat, and he cried like a child.

Miriam's death raised a public outcry against TACS and the government. Afterwards, Justice For Miriam Protests began in different Nigerian cities, and the news of her death dominated headlines for three months.

Dominic arrived in Nigeria that year and joined his brother, Patrick, to bury his sister in their family graveyard at Makurdi. The government released a statement vowing to investigate the case, but no one had heard of the TACS officer who killed Miriam since then. Dominic, via his sources, later discovered the officer was transferred to another department where he was allowed to carry out his duties undeterred.

As the years went by, Dominic's outrage against the government grew. When he went back to the United States, the only group that reached out to him was the one that started Justice for Miriam Protest. Stella Odi led it. The group would later become Justice For Miriam Foundation, headed by Stella Odi. Over the years, as Dominic and Stella's friendship grew and both became close, he'd provided the bulk of the funding the organization needed.

Dominic never forgot the evil that was done to his beloved sister. Three years after her death, he changed his identity and became Dominic Tiza. He scrubbed his past from public records, and as his tech company—Esiris grew, he began to build his new public image.

In 2016, he relocated Esiris headquarters to Nigeria. He began to appear in public—attending tech events in Lagos, Accra, Cairo, Johannesburg, and Nairobi—making speeches about the future of tech, granting interviews, and winning awards.

When the EndTACS protest began in October 2018, he and his brother joined the protest. TACS had committed lots of extra-judicial killings and atrocities, especially against the youths. The memory of the heartless killing of their sister, Miriam, by a TACS officer whom the government never punished for his crime was still fresh in the mind of the twin brothers. Government should ban TACS and punish their officers who were accused of extra-judicial killings. It was one of the requests of the youths during the protest, and Dominic believed the politicians should do the right thing.

However, things soon got out of hand when the protest took a deadly turn. Law enforcement agents began to shoot at protesters, and Dominic, Patrick, and other young people around them became angry and continued the protest while crying out against injustice.

On the twentieth of October of 2018, Dominic and Patrick joined other youths at their usual protest venue at Bendi, Lagos. They waved the country's flag and urged the government to listen to their demands. An hour later, in a sudden turn of events, law enforcement agents invaded the venue and surrounded the protesters. Then they opened fire on the unarmed citizens. What followed was a bloodbath.

Dominic watched in horror as two bullets hit his brother's chest, and he fell. Everywhere he looked, he saw many falling to their death. He ran as a stampede began. Two bullets hit his legs as he tried to climb a wall and escape. He fell and passed out.

Hours later, he opened his eyes and saw himself in a room surrounded by five people.

"God is great. He survived," they kept saying.

One of them, an elderly woman, told him how two of her children carried him out of the protest venue as he was bleeding out.

He tried to sit but couldn't. They told him they couldn't take him to the hospital because nowhere was safe. There was still panic in the country. Worse, they had covered his legs with bandages, but it was smelling. A doctor came two days later and told him the shocking news; they had to cut both his legs to save his life.

Dominic asked about his brother, but no one saw his body. He cried and agreed for the doctor to carry out the surgery. They carried him to a basement where the doctor cut both his legs. It was the worst period in his life. The family comforted him and took care of him.

Two months later, Dominic flew out of Nigeria and went back to the United States, where he went to the hospital and got further medical attention. The hospital gave him prosthetic legs and an electric wheelchair.

Over the next six months, as he watched the news, his eyes widened when he saw government officials blabbing that no protester was killed at the venue of the protest that day.

"There is no evidence of wrongdoing by the government. The alleged massacre at Bendi is a myth created by the opposition. Till now, none of them could produce the corpse of anyone killed that night."

Dominic watched from his sickbed as a government official responded to a question a journalist asked him.

As he listened to their lies on national television, he strengthened his resolve. *They will pay for their crimes,* he thought.

CHAPTER FIFTY-TWO

Dominic got temporary relief from his emotional trauma when the Nigerian government announced the formation of EndTACS Panel of Inquiry.

"This Panel will investigate reports we've received so far about crimes committed by TACS officials before and during the EndTACS protest. They will also investigate the alleged Bendi killings. If there is truth to it, all the people involved will face the wrath of the law."

Months later, he watched on national TV as a top Nigerian minister read the statement. "Be rest assured that this panel whose members are men of integrity will make sure that justice is served."

Dominic believed them and relaxed. His nightmare reduced, and he focused on expanding his business. However, his peace of mind shattered five months later when he read a press release by members of the panel who said they had finished their investigation.

"We've finished our investigation. After questioning hundreds of witnesses and doing a thorough investigation, we found the government and law enforcement officials not guilty of any wrongdoing. The Bendi Massacre is fiction. There is no evidence that any protester was killed during the protest on or before the twentieth of October."

His blood boiled from where he sat in his office. He switched off the television and smashed the television remote against the wall. For him, the next path was clear; the enemy would pay for their crimes.

He had ideas, but he needed to connect with others like him who lost their loved ones, saw what the panel of inquiry did, and would love to hit the enemy where it hurt. He almost lost hope. His turning point happened the day he shared his frustration with his close friend, Stella Odi, the founder of Justice For Miriam Foundation.

His eyes widened when Stella's face beamed, and she spoke fast. She told him about a website in the dark web where EndTACS victims met anonymously once a month to share ideas about how to exact revenge against all those who caused them pain. The website was highly protected, and its data was encrypted. Stella was one of their members. She'd lost two members of her organization during the protest.

Stella gave him a token he used to make payment and get his unique key. After going through a long verification process, he was granted access. He met young people who lost their loved ones during the Bendi Massacre and those whose friends were killed by TACS officials. He also met parents whose children were killed by TACS officials before and during the protest.

The meeting was coordinated by the Ogid, a group of twelve wealthy Nigerian citizens who had businesses and lived outside Africa. Dominic soon discovered Stella Odi was one of the members of Ogid and the only one who had an influential organization in Nigeria. It made sense how she knew so well about the website. Members of Ogid had the wealth and resources. They also had evidence of the Bendi massacre and video footage showing panel members at a round table as they collected bags of money from top government officials.

"This money will ensure that you and your children are set for life. You know what to do," one of the ministers who brought the bag of money was caught in the video speaking to the panel members.

Dominic was speechless at what he saw. The videos were played every month when the members met. After that, some would ask questions, and everyone would begin to offer ideas. Dominic had his own ideas on how to hurt the enemy the most. He shared them first with Stella, and when she told the other members of Ogid about it, they allowed it to be discussed during the following meeting.

At the next meeting, they told Dominic to share the ideas with the members, and he took his time telling them how it would work. He told them of his tech company's long-term plan to acquire Banzida—a corporation that had what they needed for the plan to work. He told them that Banzida owned Leno's Palace—a restaurant located in Nigerian Universities that catered to the children of the rich.

He shared his core idea about the plan with them. "We lost our children and loved ones during the EndTACS Protest. We were shocked when we saw members of the panel collect bribes and lie that there was no evidence that anyone was killed. Will our children die while their own children get to live?" he'd asked.

"No!" the members commented.

"To hit them hard where it hurts the most, let us target their children. When their children begin to die, they will feel our pain."

Everyone agreed, and Dominic told them more about Banzida. He'd done his research and discovered the children of the members of the EndTACS Panel of Inquiry who study in Nigerian Universities ate food at the Leno's Palace. He sought the help of Ogid.

The next time he joined other members of Ogid in their meeting online, he said, "With your help, we can acquire Banzida faster than we think and then merge it with my own company, Esiris. I will provide most of the funding, and you will join me as board members."

They agreed, and Dominic and his team worked behind the scenes to negotiate with Banzida's owner Chief Bernard Oprokoba, who was old and weak due to an illness that had ravaged his body for years. The negotiation lasted for three months before Dominic and his team finally closed the deal.

When the old man proposed to keep the sale of Banzida a secret, Dominic was okay with it. He didn't need the publicity. However, the deal leaked when both parties filed the record with the ministry of internal affairs. It generated publicity that faded after two weeks, and that was it. Dominic became Chief Executive Officer of Banzida, and Stella Odi and other members of Ogid became the corporations' top shareholders and board members.

Over the next six months, Dominic focused on transforming Leno's Palace. He optimized its operations and rebuilt its branches to have websites where students could order food online. The facelift was good for business. It set his business apart. It attracted more customers, including students with deep pockets, and gave the company more revenue.

Next, the board met and activated Project Chameleon. The plan was simple. The children of members of the panel who studied in the country's universities ate food at Leno's Palace. Dominic worked closely with the branch managers. They focused on one target at a time. They would monitor the student's movements for months before they struck.

A member of Ogid told them about a substance they would use to carry out the operation. The name was Lazine 520, a deadly, tasteless poison that could not be detected in the body. Once the target entered the restaurant and ordered food, a worker in the restaurant would put the substance in the food and offer it to the target, he or she would eat the food and go home.

The symptoms were strange and unpredictable behaviour where the victim would suddenly prefer to keep to themselves. The victim would then begin to experience rising headaches and acute depression, which would drive them to take their own life after six weeks.

A team would monitor the victim's schedule. Towards the end of the six weeks, the victim would take their life. Shortly before then, the team would hack into their smartphone and drop a Kedochat post that would make law enforcement agents and the victim's loved ones believe it was a suicide note posted by the victim.

Sometimes, the drug wasn't perfect. The timeframe was different for each of the victims but hovered between six to eight weeks. Each human body was different and unique. Some of the victims committed suicide while the drug killed other victims when the timeframe had elapsed. However, once a victim died, it would be evident to those around them that they committed suicide.

It was the perfect crime that allowed Banzida to conduct their business operations and target their victims undeterred, and under the radar without raising suspicions. As the body count mounted, members of www.cr.kt website rejoiced, and Dominic's influence among the members grew. Soon, he became their hero, and as they met each other every month, they began to adore him.

However, when the body count increased, and investigation by clueless law enforcement agents started, Dominic looked closely at the politicians and wasn't happy. Two things became clear to him; the corrupt politicians needed to feel the wrath of their anger. Second, the death of their children was not enough.

A month later, he got Intel that EndTACS Panel of Inquiry members would meet government officials and top dignitaries on the twentieth of

October to present a big book full of lies. The book the panel members planned to present recommendations they said would heal the wounds and move the country forward if they were implemented. It was bullshit. As his anger raged, an idea began to form in his mind. What if he and his team were to wipe them out on the day they would meet with the politicians while they were in that building lying to the masses?

Their deaths would grant their members justice and give them peace of mind. He knew innocent lives would be lost. It was war, and in wars, collateral damage was inevitable. This was when Project Hades was born.

When Dominic told Banzida board members about it, Stella and five members agreed. Others disagreed and insisted that they stick to the original plan of targeting the children instead of tearing the country apart. To what end?

Dominic was furious when he discovered that those who disagreed were making plans to foil Project Hades. They worked with Ken and planned to tell the authorities their well-kept secret. It would not only foil their plans, but it would also damage his reputation, lead them to their deaths and make the enemy win. He wouldn't allow that to happen. He wouldn't let the death of their loved ones be in vain. Dominic did what he had to do. He gave the order, and his team terminated the bad eggs.

He stared at the two portraits one last time and wheeled away from them. Project Hades would take place today. Nothing would stop it.

Dominic checked his wristwatch: 9:00 am. At that moment, his phone beeped. His finger tapped the screen. It was a new message.

"Sir, the event will begin by 10:00 am."

He beamed. Then, he typed, "proceed as planned" and hit send.

Time to watch them burn and continue their journey to hell. He would stay here and watch the event live as the media streamed it on national television. After the attack, he would fly out of the country and get much-needed rest after months of planning and execution. The plans had been set in motion. Once he escaped, he would hide in the deepest bowels of the world where no one would ever find him.

CHAPTER FIFTY-THREE

Ray, Sarah, Frank, and other members of DSS CID arrived at Royal Pyramid Hotel at 9.00, an hour before the event would begin. Each member of the team wore black jacket and black trousers. A bulletproof vest hugged their torsos under their jackets. They also wore a lapel mic and carried their service weapons.

The hotel was a gigantic twelve-storey building reserved for VIPs and the super-rich. It sat high at the centre of Abuja city and one kilometre away from the prestigious Eagles Square.

Even though the event was being held at the Kwame Nkrumah Conference Hall—the biggest hall at the hotel on the ground floor, the entire place was out of bounds for people who wanted to lodge at the hotel.

The white building which was full of architectural wizardly looked like something out of a science fiction movie.

It was October twentieth. The day was bright, and rays of sunshine had started streaming into the huge compound of the hotel.

Ray saw many cars coming in, including vans used by the media. He watched the security officers show the drivers where to park.

When Ray and his team stepped out of their vehicles, he observed that the whole place was patrolled by soldiers, police officers, and agents from different law enforcement agencies, who carried their service weapons.

His boss had already briefed them on what to expect. Gideon had told them that all security personnel in the building reported to three officers.

The moment they walked past the metal gate and entered the compound, they met the three men in uniform in charge of the security detail for the event.

Ray shook hands with the first officer, Lawrence Vasni. From the brief dossier he'd read, he knew he was the Deputy Inspector General of Police.

"I'm Ray," he said and greeted him.

The officer flashed him a warm smile. "Call me Lawrence. I've heard great things about you. It's a pleasure to meet you here." Lawrence gave him a firm handshake and flashed his yellow teeth.

The next officer was Alex Inibehe. Alex was light-skinned, slim, and of average height. His face was spotty with acne.

Lawrence introduced his colleague, "Meet Alex. He is a police officer working in the Operations Unit of Police Headquarters here in Abuja."

Ray greeted him.

"Meet Lt. Col. Jeremiah Okoh. He is a security reconnaissance expert in Defence Headquarters here in Abuja," Lawrence said.

Both men shook hands with Ray.

"It's great to see you and your team here, Ray," the lieutenant colonel said. Then he cracked a joke, and they all laughed.

Ray liked him instantly. He was dark-skinned, six feet tall, and appeared to be in his early forties. Ray felt he was easy-going. He watched the rest of the team greet the three officers. The moment the greetings and exchange of pleasantries ended, Sarah, standing beside Ray, asked Lawrence Vasni, "Officer, can this event be called off?"

Lawrence shook his head and said, "We can't call it off, and we won't. We have heard your worries that this building will be attacked today. It's not possible. Our people patrol every corner of this building. We check everything, including the dustbin."

Lt. Col. Jeremiah chipped in, "Since this building was chosen as the venue for this event three weeks ago, we've set up strict security protocol. We can see everything that comes in and goes out of this building."

"Security cameras are everywhere, and our people monitor them every second," Alex said.

"Our people scan everywhere, including all vehicles, with police dogs, interceptors, and jammers. This place is more secure than a fortress. Nothing takes place without our permission. We will ensure the safety of everyone that will come for this great event today. So, Ray, you and your team have no reason to panic," Lawrence explained.

Ray and the rest of his team asked further questions about the event and how well prepared the security detail was. The officers answered calmly, providing all the details they needed.

His observation was that they were highly organized. Of course, the president, members of the federal executive council, and top dignitaries would be here today. He didn't expect less from them.

When Ray and his team finished speaking with them, they walked through the metal detector and entered through the golden oak-panelled door of Kwame Nkrumah Hall. The hall was magnificent. Gold-coloured chandeliers hung from the ceilings. Huge HD flat screens hung at the different sides of the venue, showing everything going on inside. They were streamed live on National Television Stations to the audiences watching from all over the world.

Two governors trouped in with their entourage. Ray saw an NTA journalist interviewing a member of the House of Representatives whose white *Agbada* outfit touched the floor. Everything seemed okay.

When he checked the time, it was 9:15 am. The event would begin in forty-five minutes.

CHAPTER FIFTY-FOUR

Sarah Aderinsola walked briskly towards the second gate, her face tight, eyes capturing the tiniest details. A male channel TV reporter saw her and rushed towards her. She forced a smile and waved him off. "Please, I can't talk now.'

She saw a hint of disappointment in the eyes of the young reporter. He must've been promoted and wanted to impress his new bosses. He nodded and went away. She didn't need the distraction; she needed to focus. She'd felt the wrath of Banzida when they'd shot her and left her for dead. She still felt pain in her chest since the attack took place. Banzida seemed to be a step ahead. This time, she was determined to work with the agents there and ensure Banzida failed.

From where she stood at the second gate, she observed police officers scanning each vehicle before giving the drivers a gold-plated card that would allow them to enter through the gate. Other police officers were in different sections of the big compound directing the vehicles and showing them where to park.

Since she arrived at the hotel, she'd watched the guests and dignitaries as they trooped into the building for the day's event. She'd been scanning the faces of everyone and hadn't noticed anything amiss. At that moment, streaks of sunlight hit her face, blinding her temporarily. She stepped back into the compound and watched as the doors of a white SUV and black Lexus jeep opened.

The drivers opened the back door of their vehicles. Senator Magu, chairman of EndTACS Panel of Inquiry, stepped out of his SUV and greeted Stephen Abada, former Inspector General of Police, as he alighted from his black Lexus jeep. They wore white *Agbada*. Both men were members of the panel and had lost their children.

The men shook hands firmly. The former Inspector General of Police whispered something in Senator Magu's ear, and he laughed. Over the next ten minutes, Sarah watched as more members of the panel entered the hall. Among them were Honourable Badmus Onyeama, Senator David Adebayo, Simon Okafor, and the four female members of the committee.

Simon Okafor and Senator David Adebayo wore sad faces. They appeared to be the only members of the panel mourning the tragic loss of their loved ones.

Sarah took her eyes off the guests and saw Ray in an animated conversation with Lawrence. Lawrence kept nodding while he listened to Ray.

She liked how the security detail operated with a high level of professionalism. The minutes flew as she continued her work. Then, when she looked up again, she saw Ray walking toward her.

"Notice anything suspicious?" Ray asked as he joined her at the second gate.

"None. Everything appears serene. Nothing is out of place," Sarah said, and both watched the rest of the compound in silence.

A thought hit her. The enemy had always been one step ahead. What were they planning? Filled with frustration, she watched as top dignitaries entered the building. This time, it was top politicians, ministers, members of the press, and members of civil society organizations.

Six minutes later, Alex called her, and she left Ray and joined him. Both began to act as ushers leading the VIPs inside the hall and showing them to their reserved seats. When she finished helping five southern governors, she walked toward the entrance. But she stopped when she heard Senator Magu's voice in the microphone.

"Ladies and gentlemen, we ..."

She checked her watch. 10:00 am. The event had started.

CHAPTER FIFTY-FIVE

Senator Vincent Magu lifted his long-flowing *Agbada* dress from the ground and waved to the guests in the hall as he walked to the podium. When he reached the platform, he greeted other members of the panel, put his chubby face in front of an array of microphones attached to the stage, and smiled as camera lights hit his face.

After weeks of mourning the death of his only son, this event had brought him back to the limelight. As chairman of the panel, it was his duty to ensure the committee did their job effectively. His sad, afflicted mood had vanished within minutes of entering the building and greeting his colleagues and other dignitaries. He'd quickly settled into doing what he loved to do most.

He smiled as he scanned the faces of the guests waiting to hear what he had to say. The feeling made him confident and powerful. He'd received the news that the president and vice president would be there in twenty minutes, and he looked forward to it.

He brought out a big book bounded in thick hardcover and covered in white and green. The title of the book 'Beyond The EndTACS Protest: The

Road To A Viable Nationhood' was boldly inscribed with giant letters on the front cover.

He began to speak, "Ladies and gentlemen, today is a great day in the history of our country. I thank the EndTACS Panel of Inquiry members for their splendid work for our country. The EndTACS protest has come and gone, but our youths are still nursing old wounds. It's understandable. However, it's time for us to put bad memories in the past where they belong and work together to build a great nation for our children. The panel members have worked hard to create a permanent solution to the problems threatening our nationhood. After months of hard work, I'm glad to announce that our panel have produced a book. This book contains recommendations on key resolutions we made during our investigation of the EndTACS Protest. The recommendations offer our country a clear path to a viable nationhood. We…"

***

Ray watched Senator Magu speak passionately about the work he and his panel had done. At that instant, he heard Lawrence's voice on the lapel mic.

"Blue Whale One and Blue Whale Two are on their way. They will be here in twenty minutes."

Those were code names for the president and the vice president.

"Got it," Ray replied and moved through the crowd.

He scanned the environment, but everything seemed all right, like a typical day in Abuja. As he moved through the building, his gaze met a pregnant journalist carrying a child. Sweat was on her face as she sat in her seat and listened to Senator Magu's speech. A boy of about five years old sat beside his father. Worry crept up his spine when he saw a group of people sitting at the end of the hall. They were members of civil society organizations waiting for the book to be unveiled. He looked around and saw reporters, their cameras capturing the senator's face.

Ray believed the young people were right to tell the government about their demands when starting the EndTACS Protest. He knew TACS had hurt young people over the past decade. The video footage of TACS members harassing young people during the protests made him weep. He believed the government should shut down the controversial police unit guilty of extortion, injustice and killing young and unarmed people.

As a DSS Agent, he always did his job and served his country wholeheartedly. He'd never forgotten his duty to the nation: maintain law and order, keep the criminals away and citizens safe. Unfortunately, most TACS officials did the opposite. They harassed the citizens without probable cause, especially successful youths who lived good lives—as though looking good and living a good life as a young person was a crime. Over the years, they became the monsters against which they were fighting.

Ray knew most politicians in the country were corrupt. Every day, the politicians' bribery and corruption made headlines in national newspapers. The same corrupt politicians also became members of the EndTACS Panel of Inquiry.

However, in a court of law, one would have to present evidence before he'd condemn another as guilty. What Dominic Tiza endured was heart-breaking. But he and his cohorts should not be the judge, jury, and executioner in their quest for revenge.

Ray glanced around the hall. The clock was ticking. They could not call off the event. They had twenty minutes to terminate Project Hades, or everyone in the building, including all those innocent people, would die.

CHAPTER FIFTY-SIX

Ray watched as Senator Magu finished his speech, followed by a standing ovation. He greeted other panel members and hugged Mrs Stella Oyedele, one of the prominent members of the panel and a former speaker of the House of Representatives.

Frank joined him five minutes later, and they watched the proceedings together.

A minute later, Simon Okafor, a member of the panel and former chief justice of the Appeal Court, began to speak. "Ladies and gentlemen, on this historic occasion...."

Ray hadn't heard him speak before. His voice was calm and steady. Wire-rimmed glasses covered his face.

Ray checked the time. Fifteen minutes before the president and his vice would arrive. He and his team members had done a thorough check of the building. He'd played and dismissed so many scenarios in his mind. His gut told him there was something critical they were missing.

"What if Banzida is using a suicide bomb?" Frank asked.

The question dropped like a thud in Ray's mind. Its possibility was difficult to ignore. He hadn't considered this. He knew Dominic Tiza could go to any length to carry out the attack.

"How will they get the suicide bomber inside the building?" he asked.

"He or she could be one of the police officers patrolling this building right now."

"And the jammers and interceptor will fail to intercept the bombers?" he asked, but Frank remained silent.

His eyes scanned the building. Even as Ray doubted it, a part of him told him it was possible. Searching for a suicide bomber among the security agents and the people in the building was like looking for a needle in a haystack.

At that moment, Sarah's voice cracked in his lapel mic. "Ray, I just saw him in a military uniform.

Ray stood alert. He tapped Frank's right shoulder.

Frank saw the serious expression on his face and came close.

"Who?" asked Ray.

"Bruno Tema. I think he and his men are here disguised as soldiers."

"What did Sarah say?" Frank asked, his face conjugated with worry as they started heading in Sarah's direction.

"She said she saw Bruno Tema. She believes he and his team are here," Ray replied.

Frank clenched his fist. "How did they get in?"

This was the same question in Ray's mind. So many ideas ran through his mind. How did they do it? Perhaps, they planned to open fire on everyone in the building at the right time. The right time—he presumed would be when the president and his vice had arrived, and they would be there shortly.

No one would suspect Bruno and his men because they were dressed as soldiers and deserved to carry weapons. Another question tugged at the back of his mind as they left the building and approached the second gate where Sarah was working. Were they part of a new security detail that entered the compound recently?

Sarah watched a group of soldiers standing at the compound's right-hand side.

"Where is he?" Frank asked the moment they met Sarah.

"He has entered the hall," Sarah said.

Ray's eyes widened.

"Follow me."

They followed her and walked inside the hall.

"Look ahead. 90 degrees. Dark-skinned man. Six feet tall. Broad shoulders. He is wearing a military uniform. Blended in perfectly."

Ray spotted him. They could only see his back. They walked towards him, pushing through the crowd as the voice of a former president boomed in the overhead speakers.

"Hey." Frank tapped the soldier's arm.

The soldier was watching the speaker intently. His pose and unusual curiosity were suspicious. He turned and faced them as surprise registered on his face. When Ray saw the man's face, he knew he wasn't Bruno Tema.

***

Ray read the name tag on his right shoulder, 'Captain Michael Nwosu.'

"We are sorry. We thought you were someone else," Ray apologized.

The soldier waved it off. "It's alright. No offence taken."

As they left, guilt clogged Ray's throat for what they had just done. They needed to be careful. When they reached the end of the hall, he checked the time. It was ten minutes until the president and his vice arrived. He stared at the door and saw young men and women carrying white boxes and walking towards a table close to the podium.

"These are copies of the book written by the panel. The president will be here in ten minutes to cut the tape and officially unveil the book. Afterwards, the book presentation will begin," Sarah explained. She looked at their faces. "I'm sorry for leading you guys on a wild goose chase."

"You don't have to apologize. It's good to be cautious," Frank reassured her.

Ray nodded, agreeing with Frank.

He was uncomfortable. He stared at his wristwatch again and saw time slipping away. Project Hades. It was now nine minutes to the dreaded apocalypse. How did Banzida plan to do this? His mind came up empty. As he watched the young men and women drop the books cartons on the table, the answer he sought hit him hard like a blinding light.

"Oh my God. This is it!"

"What?" Frank and Sarah said at the same time.

"The heads of the security detail," Ray said.

"The three leaders. What about them?" Frank asked.

"Everyone reports to them. They check and supervise everything and everyone. They have been doing this since the day this building was chosen as the venue for this event," Ray said.

Sarah's eyes narrowed. Ray figured she understood what he meant.

"They check and monitor everyone else, but who checks them?" Sarah asked.

"No one. They are the ones who set the rules, and they know all the loopholes to the rules they set," Frank added.

They have figured it out, Ray thought as the implication of what they had overlooked since they arrived made him tighten his fists. It was time to find out who among the three leaders of the security detail was working for the enemy.

CHAPTER FIFTY-SEVEN

Frank and Sarah joined Ray as they walked through the crowd, searching for the first man, Lawrence Vasni.

"I just saw him now. Look to your left," Frank said.

Ray and Sarah followed his gaze. Lawrence was giving orders to his men. The three agents observed him.

"Lawrence Vasni is the Deputy Inspector General of Police. He is the youngest to attain that position in the history of the Nigerian Police Force. He has thirty-four years of experience in the force and will retire next year. Lawrence is the only child of his parents. His parents were killed in Jos in 2002," Sarah explained.

Ray knew Lawrence's impressive resume. His parents were killed during the infamous bomb attack in Jos in 2002. Was he blaming the government for losing his parents? Had he been nursing this grudge since 2002? This was a good motive for an officer of his position to work for the enemy.

Lawrence suddenly turned and waved at them with a warm smile. They greeted him. Lawrence moved away from where he stood and approached a female journalist who asked him for directions.

They moved on to the second man. They saw him directing vehicles at the second gate of the building.

"Lt. Col. Jeremiah Okoh is a security reconnaissance expert in defence headquarters. He has worked in the military for twenty-six years. My sources at NIA said he has a clean record. He was a part of the Nigerian soldiers that fought during the war in Liberia," Sarah said.

"The ECOMOG contingent," Frank chirped in.

"Yes. In 2012, he successfully led his team to nullify a Boko Haram planned attack at Maiduguri. He is married with three kids," Sarah said.

Ray observed the lieutenant colonel closely. He didn't smile, but his professionalism and military training showed.

They moved on to the third man, Alex Onihebe. They spotted him standing at the entrance to the hall. He was engaged in a conversation with two junior police officers. He whispered something to them, and they nodded.

"Alex is the one with the best record. Apart from being a handsome police officer, he is a building security expert, one of the best in the country. He studied security and strategic planning at Harvard. He taught at Nigerian Police Academy for three years before being promoted to Chief Superintendent of Police at the age of twenty-five. Afterwards, he was posted to work at the Nigerian Police Force Headquarters operations unit here in

Abuja. He has been there ever since," Sarah explained.

Ray saw Alex smiling and shaking hands with dignitaries.

"Great guy," Frank observed.

Ray thought so too.

CHAPTER FIFTY-EIGHT

The three agents continued to watch Alex. After a short while, Ray checked his watch; it was seven minutes until the president and vice arrived. Alex greeted a female journalist, then briefly checked his watch, and continued his conversation with the journalist. It was a normal thing to do, but alarm bells rang in Ray's ears.

Alex fixed his gaze at the hall's front door, and a sad expression appeared on his face. It vanished quickly and was replaced with a smile. Ray's eyes narrowed. Did he imagine it? His mind told him something was terribly wrong, and Alex knew the answer.

"Alex," Ray said

"What?" Sarah and Frank asked in unison.

Ray alerted other members of their DSS CID team, who joined them two minutes later. He told them his plan, and they agreed. They walked towards Alex. When they reached where he was, Frank tapped his shoulder. "One minute, Alex."

Alex turned and stared at them. "I'm busy. The president will soon be here." He paused, and his expression softened. "It's alright. What is it?" He turned and apologized to the journalist. "I'm so sorry, Linda. We will have this conversation another time."

"Thank you, Alex," the journalist said.

Ray led the way and walked through the door to an empty corridor. Alex followed them. When they reached the middle of the hallway, Ray stopped and said, "Alex, we need to search you."

A frown marred Alex's handsome face. "What are you talking about?" Are you out of your mind?"

"Alex, you have nothing to worry about if you don't have anything to hide," Frank assured him.

Alex fumed. "I will report all of you. This is preposterous." He raised his hand after speaking.

Sarah and Frank searched him and came up empty. "We found nothing on him. He is squeaky clean," Sarah said, admiring Alex's features and artfully carved goatee.

Ray thought about the brief sadness he saw at the corner of Alex's eyes, one of the many micro facial expressions they were taught to detect while studying at the DSS Academy in Lagos. His gut told him he hadn't imagined it.

"Alex, we want to ask you some questions, but this is not the right place." Ray stared at the corridor close to the noisy hall where the event was taking place.

Frank said, "Alex, let's get out of this building. We don't want to raise unnecessary panic."

"No, what is the meaning of this?" Alex protested. He calmed down when he saw the serious expression on their faces.

They took him out of the building and led him to Ray's Toyota. Sarah rushed and opened the passenger door for him. As he was about to enter the car, his head exploded, and his body slumped to the ground. A second bullet shattered the vehicle's windscreen. Ray and his team dived into the nearby bush across the gutter.

***

At the same time, a few buildings away, a man in a black shirt, jeans, and black face mask began to loosen his high calibre rifle, his expert fingers moving with deadly efficiency. Within seconds, he put the parts of the gun inside a thick black laptop bag. He was inside a three-storey building that was directly opposite the hotel. He could see the front gate clearly and the panic and confusion he had triggered.

He saw pot-bellied politicians scrambling out of the building with their bodyguards. He saw a DSS agent who rushed into the hall. Other agents, soldiers, and police officers followed him. This place was no longer safe for him. He needed to leave after making a phone call.

He brought out his scrambler phone and placed a call to a man who was watching the whole event unfold on his television screen. When he heard the five-second hum, he waited. The phone rang for three seconds more before Dominic Tiza answered the call.

"Go ahead."

"Alex has been terminated. He's no longer a threat."

"Leave the building right now and go back to your location."

"Yes, sir." He heard a click that told him the call had ended.

He slung his bag over his shoulder and walked to the elevator that would take him out of the building. From there, he'd merge with the panicking crowd and use the rare opportunity the chaos he caused had provided him to escape.

CHAPTER FIFTY-NINE

The moment Ray and his team members rose from where they lay on the ground, they rushed inside the compound. Ray watched as people scrambled out of the building. He quickly collected a portable microphone from a police officer and said, "Code red. There is a security breach. Everyone should leave the building now!"

He returned the microphone and saw Lawrence Vasni's concerned face as he rushed towards him.

"Thank God you guys are not hurt," Lawrence said and stared at the shattered body of his colleague, which lay on the ground. "Oh God, Alex."

The clock was ticking. Ray knew they had to move fast. They'd suspected Alex was the leak. Banzida killed him before he could talk, which meant they were here, and Ray and his team were correct. The implication of what this meant was clear to him.

He stared at Lawrence. "Tell the security team bringing the president and his vice to take them back to the Presidential Palace, Aso Rock. This place is not safe."

"Yes, sir," Lawrence said and rushed to make calls.

Ray watched as chaos and panic seized the whole building. The dignitaries scrambled for safety with their bodyguards, who escorted them to their cars.

"It might be a bomb," Sarah said.

"I think so too. We need to find the bomb and deactivate it, so it doesn't blow up the building," Ray said, and they both rushed into the hall.

They began searching all corners of the building. Ray was worried if it was really a bomb, no one would know when it would blow off. An agent working with Banzida might set it off any moment from now.

***

Sarah, Ray, and the rest of the security team searched the venue and came up empty. Sarah was breathless as fatigue plagued her body. Lt. Col. Jeremiah had ordered soldiers and police officers to search every room in the hotel. No one had found anything yet. She entered a mezzanine level other officers had already explored, accessible by stairs. When the hall was filled with guests, others would sit there to watch the show in the main hall.

A faint beeping sound came from the ceiling, which was within arm's reach. Her heart raced as she found a hammer lying across the tiled floor. She grabbed it and slammed it hard against the ceiling. It shattered. She stared at the opening and gasped.

A maze of C-4 explosives had a red dot flashing every second at the centre of the panel, which had a sophisticated electrical connection.

She covered her mouth with her hand. "Oh my God!"

At that moment, Ray joined her. "Sarah, what is…."

Both stared at the time, which was counting down. 7:30 minutes remained.

Sarah and Ray began calling for help.

CHAPTER SIXTY

Sarah held Ray's hand as three bomb specialists rushed into that side of the building. From their uniform, she knew they were members of the military. The lead man, Jaba Mustapha, was tall and had a prominent nose.

They used a bench to climb so they could see the explosive clearly. The three men wore gloves. Jaba held a pair of fabric scissors while the two other men beside him pointed torchlight at the pack of explosives.

The rest of the security teams joined them and watched with faces sagging with anguish.

"Jaba, what do you see?" Lawrence Vasni said.

"Lots of C-4 explosives."

"Whoever did this made sure that when the bombs explode, it will raze down the whole building and kill everyone inside," Jaba observed.

Sarah tightened her grip on Ray's hand as Jaba began to cut through the plastic covering of the panel. When he removed it, they gasped when they saw an array of wires; the time remaining was one minute, thirty seconds.

"I can see the power source," Jaba announced.

"Careful, Jaba, any mistake and the whole building will explode," Jaba's partner said.

Sarah saw the sweat on Jaba's face and mouthed a brief prayer.

"Time to defuse the bomb," Jaba said.

Everyone watched intently. The time remaining was fifty-nine seconds.

Jaba carefully separated two wires. One was blue, the other red. He used the scissors to cut the red wire, and the clock stopped at 30 seconds. Everyone released a deep sigh of relief.

***

After members of the bomb squad had disarmed and dismantled the bombs, Ray joined other members of the security detail to clear the building of the remaining guests. Afterwards, he met Lawrence when he entered the hall and said, "Where can we locate the control centre which houses the video footage from the security cameras?"

Lawrence gave him the directions. "Walk straight. Once you reach the stage, look ahead. You will see room three. That's the control centre."

Ray alerted his team members, and they joined him at the centre of the hall. From there, they advanced with long strides to the control centre.

***

The police officer in the control centre room was a short and dark-skinned man named Bob. He sat in a swivel chair where he could watch HD TV screens that captured different video footage from security cameras planted in the hall and various parts of the building. An empty seat was beside him.

Ray and members of his team greeted him when they entered.

"I guess this empty seat is for your partner. Where is he?" Frank asked.

Bob said, "Our boss called him. He joined the rest of our team to search the building."

By their boss, Ray knew he meant Lawrence Vasni. He explained to Bob what they needed.

Bob nodded, tapped the keyboard, and different video footage appeared on the screen. "Where do you want to start?" he asked Ray.

"Start from the first day, the day this building was chosen as the venue for the event."

He nodded again and clicked play on one of the videos.

"You can take a seat," he said to them and pointed at the plastic chairs in the room. They each took a plastic chair and sat close to him as he fast-forwarded the videos.

For two hours, they didn't see anything out of place. Then, Bob increased the speed, and the video footage moved faster. Ray watched as the date in the video changed and the day of the event drew nearer.

"Stop!" Sarah's voice boomed.

Bob paused the video, and everyone looked closely.

Ray saw people carrying canopy and large sets of clothes. From the date on the screen, he knew this took place on the sixteenth of October, four days before the event began.

"They are the people that decorated the hall."

In the video, police officers stopped them. They searched and inspected their materials. When they reached the entrance to the hall, they went through a metal detector and were cleared to go in.

Ray sighed as Bob clicked play, and they kept watching. Two questions were on his mind, how did Banzida bring the bombs inside the building? How did they avoid detection?

He fixed his gaze at the screen as the questions played in his mind.

"Stop!" he shouted. The video was playing fast, but he saw something that caught his attention.

Everyone became alert, and Bob paused the video. In the video footage, a white bus stopped outside the gate, and the driver wearing clothes with the AEDC logo climbed down from the vehicle.

"What's AEDC?" A member of the team asked.

"Abuja Electricity Distribution Company. This is the company that supplies electricity to Abuja. Those are their workers. That day, they came and installed an electricity pole and fixed the electricity problem in the building," Bob explained.

Ray stared at the date in the video footage, the seventeenth of October, three days before the event.

They watched as the driver spoke with a police officer, and he waved at them to go in.

"What is going on here? No one inspected them?" Sarah observed.

Ray's eyes narrowed. The driver climbed back into his vehicle and entered the compound. "Who is that police officer giving them the order to go in?" Ray asked.

"That's strange. We don't do this. The officer was wrong. I didn't notice this before," Bob said. A deep frown drew lines on his temple.

At that moment, the police officer who gave the order turned, and the camera captured his face.

"Alex Inibehe," Sarah said matter-of-factly.

Ray froze. He watched as junior police officers stood at attention as Alex talked to them. He was their boss, and they would do anything he ordered them to do.

In the video footage, Alex walked briskly to the hall's front door and opened it. Five men wearing AEDC uniforms stepped out of the bus. They carried a set of electric wires and two black bags. One of them touched Alex on the shoulder, and the camera captured his face, which was covered by a face cap.

"Pause the video and zoom that image," Ray said.

Bob paused the video and zoomed in on the face of the man in the AEDC uniform.

"Oh my God, that's Bruno Tema," Sarah gasped.

Ray watched as Bruno and his men entered the hall through the door.

He stared at Bob. "You missed this. Who was here that day?"

"We work on shifts. My partner, Damon, was the one in charge that day."

"Where is he now?"

"He joined other...."

Ray stared at Frank and other members of his team. "Find Damon." He glanced at Sarah. "Stay here."

Frank nodded.

As his team members were leaving, Ray pressed Lawrence's number, and they spoke briefly. Five minutes later, Lawrence entered the control room, his face clogged with exhaustion

He watched as Bob replayed that section of the video footage for him.

"Oh God, Alex. I still can't believe it. He is a saint at police headquarters," Lawrence said as his wide eyes were glued to the screen.

"It's clear that this was how Banzida planted the bombs in the building," Sarah said.

"Yes, they were working with someone on the inside, Alex Inibehe," Ray said.

"Unfortunately, Alex is dead. If he was alive, he would have given us answers. So, we are back to square one," Sarah said, and Ray collapsed in his seat.

At that moment, Ray's phone rang, and he answered the call.

"Ray, Damon is not here. He's gone," Frank said, his voice unsteady.

Ray ended the call and put his phone in his pocket. He told them what Frank said.

"I will look into this. I can't believe all of this is happening," Lawrence said, his eyes dazed with shock.

"We need to stop Banzida. We need to find them, but a nationwide hunt will not be effective," Sarah said.

Ray glanced at Lawrence. "Sir, what do you know about Alex? What about his family?"

"Alex is social but keeps to himself. He lives with his wife in Lagos," Lawrence replied.

Ray glanced at Sarah. "We need to question his wife."

CHAPTER SIXTY-ONE

Ray and Sarah travelled back to Lagos. Frank and other team members stayed in Abuja and planned to get to Lagos the following day. Fear gripped the whole nation. News headlines captured details about the averted attack.

As they climbed down from the plane, Ray picked up a newspaper. Then, when they entered the Sienna vehicle the agency arranged for them, he stared at one of the headlines.

A planned bomb attack against the president and top dignitaries was averted at the last minute by members of the security detail assigned to the event led by Deputy Inspector General of Police, Lawrence Vasni.

Ray narrowed his eyes.

"Is that so? It's obvious he has taken the credit," Sarah said as she read the headlines.

Let them take the credit, Ray thought. He preferred to stay behind the scenes and do his work without disturbance.

The driver of the Sienna dropped them outside a white gate in Ikoyi, and they climbed down from the vehicle.

When they entered the compound and gave their names to the gate keeper, Ray took his time observing Alex Inibehe's house. The bungalow was painted off-white. Two Toyotas covered with yellow tarpaulin sat close to the wall. He glanced at the well-trimmed flowers at the centre of the cemented compound.

A minute later, the door opened, and a tall, dark-skinned woman appeared. Her eyes were puffy, and her face tight. Ray guessed she had heard about her husband's death. He wondered what the police had told her.

He flashed his badge and explained who they were. "We are sorry for your loss."

"We would like you to help us clear your late husband's name," Sarah said.

Ray saw her suspicious eyes change, and curiosity covered her face. "Madam, we'd like to ask you a few questions," he said.

"Akpan, go back to the gate," she said to the gateman.

When he left, she stared at them and opened the door. "Come inside."

When they took their seats on the couch in the living room, Sarah began to ask her a series of questions.

"I have no idea what you are talking about," the woman said.

When Sarah wanted to speak again, Ray signalled her with his eyes to keep quiet. He brought out a brown envelope. "Madam, what did the police tell you about your husband's death?"

Tears filled the woman's eyes. "They said he was killed during the attack by the people behind it. They said he died a hero."

Ray stared at her and considered his next statement. "We would like it to remain that way."

The woman frowned. "What do you mean?"

Ray brought pictures from the video footage of Alex with Bruno and his team. He showed her more photos of Alex working with Banzida. "Madam, the police didn't tell you the truth. Your husband was working with the enemy. We have Intel showing that he invited them inside the hall. They disguised as AEDC workers and used the opportunity to plant the bombs that would have razed down that building and killed everyone," he said.

"We figured your husband was the leak minutes before the president was scheduled to arrive. When we led him out of the building to question him, a Banzida operative took him out before he could talk to us. That was how he died," Sarah chipped in.

The woman's mouth hung open as Ray showed her pictures of her late husband with members of Banzida.

"Madam, we need your help in this investigation. We need to catch these people. For your co-operation, we will ensure your husband isn't revealed as a traitor. He was lured into this by Banzida operatives," Ray said.

Mrs Inibehe remained quiet for a while. When she finally lifted her gaze to Ray, she said, "A woman visited my late husband twice in this house. Anytime she comes, they would stay for twenty minutes in his study." She began to sob.

Ray and Sarah became alert.

"Please, go on," Sarah said.

"He receives visitors every time, but this one was strange," she said

"Who is this woman?"

"I don't know who she is. But during her second visit, I began to suspect that my husband was cheating on me. Then, I snapped a picture of her as she was leaving the house." She brought out her phone and showed them the photo.

Ray's eyes widened. The picture only showed part of her face, but it rang a bell in his mind.

"I've seen this woman before on TV," Sarah said.

Ray had seen her on TV too. He switched on the Bluetooth of his phone and told Mrs Inibehe to send the picture to him. When she did as instructed, they greeted her and left the house.

Who was that woman? They needed to find out.

**

At 10:00 am the next day, Ray and Sarah joined Gideon Owolabi, Steve Maccido, Christine Zainab, and Frank Igwe for a meeting in a conference room at the DSS Lagos branch. Everyone watched intently as Christine ran the photograph on the agency's facial recognition software. A minute later, a picture that matched it by 99.9 percent, along with a name, appeared on the screen. Everyone in the room gasped.

"Her name is Stella Odi," Christine said.

"Do you mean Stella Odi, the founder of Justice for Miriam Foundation?" Frank asked.

"Yes, and it gets worse. ₦100 million entered Alex's bank account on October ten. It came from a series of fake shell corporations. I followed the trail and traced it to Stelinbell, a company in Dubai owned by Stella Odi," Christine explained.

"This is serious," Steve said, his expression tight.

"It doesn't end there. Stella and the CEO of Banzida, Dominic Tiza, have known each other for years," Christine said.

Everyone watched in surprise as Christine showed them pictures of Stella and Dominic at parties and events they had attended over the years.

"They have always been together. We missed this during the investigation," Christine said. "That's not all. I have a record showing they were classmates at the same secondary school in Makurdi."

She tapped some keys on her keyboard, and an image appeared on the screen.

Ray narrowed his eyes and read the names. It was from a class register at St. Stephen's Secondary School, Makurdi, dated 1999.

"Stella may be a member of Banzida," Sarah said.

"Where is Stella now?" Gideon asked, his face laced with anger.

Christine removed her eyes from the screen and stared at them. "She probably believes no one would ever detect her involvement with Banzida. Her address is in the public record. She lives in Banana Island here in Lagos."

CHAPTER SIXTY-TWO

Several thoughts ran into Ray's mind as he sat beside Sarah in the backseat of the Toyota. Frank Igwe, Chris Oluyemi, and Clement Emori were in the second Toyota, which followed them closely. The agents wore black bulletproof vest and trousers and communicated via the lapel mic.

Stella Odi. He'd read so much about her heroics in the last three hours. *What a character.* He was no longer surprised. This case had taken him on a journey he would never forget. He was determined to see it through to the end.

When they entered Ikoyi, the driver drove through Kingsway Road to Gerrard Road. They went through the beautiful Modupe Alakija Crescent and entered First Avenue in Banana Island six minutes later.

Banana Island was an area of Ikoyi, 8.6 kilometres east of Tafewa Balewa square. The island was known for its wealthy community and had some of Nigeria's most expensive real estate. As their vehicles moved at a slower speed, they were greeted by the sight of the well-laid lawns, beautiful towers, and well-paved roads. Beautiful trees were planted in canopy form to serve as an umbrella and supply fresh air.

The driver passed First Avenue, took a left, and stopped in front of a duplex covered with Italian tiles. "This is the address," he said.

Ray stared at the paper he held in his hands and nodded. "Yes, this is where Stella Odi lives."

He began to give orders to his men.

***

Stella Odi fumed angrily as she watched the news in her living room. At thirty-six, she was stunning, and her beauty was irresistible. Her house was state of the art and furnished to her taste. Her conservative blue hip-hugging gown contrasted the expensive furniture and painting she used to decorate her house. However, her dress complemented her light-skinned complexion.

She was a powerful woman who had created a legacy and made a name for herself as the voice of the hopeless and champion of justice. Now it pained her that one terrible mistake she'd made in her life threatened to shatter everything she'd built.

She tapped a key on the laptop, which sat on a glass table beside her, and narrowed her eyes when she discovered she had a new email. Reading the email filled her with rage. She hit the keyboard with fast fingers as she replied.

Suddenly, her doorbell rang, and she rose from her seat and went to unlock the door. The moment she unlocked it, it flung open, and she watched in horror as DSS agents entered her living room and surrounded her. A dark-skinned, athletic DSS agent who appeared to be their leader approached her. "Stella Odi, you are under arrest for murder and treason. You have the right to remain silent. Anything you say here can be used against you in the court of law."

***

The moment Ray read her Miranda rights, Stella broke into laughter. When she stopped, anger laced her face. "What is the meaning of this? Agents of the State. Tools of oppression. A desperate tactic by a corrupt government. This is harassment, and I will sue you in court for abusing my rights." Her authoritative voice shook the entire room.

Ray signalled his team. Chris and Clement handcuffed her, dragging her out of the building.

***

Sweat covered Stella Odi's face as she sat handcuffed inside the interrogation room at the DSS Lagos branch office building. Ray, Frank, and Sarah sat in front of her.

In an interrogation that lasted for three hours, Stella watched as a series of evidence presented by Ray and his team made her speechless and limited her options.

Ray showed her how the attack was planned and how they stopped it. He showed her the financial records and how she paid a hundred million naira to Alex Inibehe, money they traced back to her Dubai-based company—Stelinbell.

They showed her a photograph of her in Alex Inibehe's house, which was taken by the wife of the late police officer.

"Madam," Ray said, "For the last time, tell us everything you know or face the death penalty."

"I don't want to die, please," Stella said and began to sob.

Ray became silent and listened as Stella finally began to talk.

"I loved him, and that mistake affected my sense of judgment," Stella said.

"To be clear, 'by him,' you mean Dominic Tiza, is that correct?" Frank asked.

Stella nodded and continued, "I took his late sister's case personally and every other cause he believed in."

Ray cut in. "By his late sister, you mean Miriam Tersoo, is that correct?"

"Yes," Stella said. "I had a crush on him since we were in secondary school. However, her sister's death presented a unique opportunity. It was horrible and wrong. She deserved justice. We were right to protest and call the world's attention to the ills of the TACS police unit. The movement we started in 2011 gave me the momentum I used to launch Justice For Miriam Foundation. Miriam's death enabled me to carefully enter Dominic's life.

"But despite everything I did for him, he only saw me as a friend. Dominic is wealthy but broken. He is obsessed with building the next tech gadget and achieving his endless thirst for revenge. Unfortunately, he doesn't want the love of a woman. I'm tired of compromising my principles to feed his lust for revenge. Over the years, since I got close to him, determined to make him accept my love for him, I have morphed into a creature I can't recognize." She paused and stared at Ray. "The world knows me as a champion of justice, but I have done horrible things for Dominic and Banzida. I am tired." She sobbed harder, and the tears on her cheeks smeared the mascara on her face.

Ray's heart raced as Stella continued to talk. She told them she was a member of Ogid, the highest decision-making body at Banzida and www.cr.kt—the website on the dark web where their members meet and plan how to hurt their enemies.

"We were the ones that put Project Hades in motion. Our plan was to make the enemy pay for their crimes. I was the one who got to Alex. I knew his story. He was stuck in the rat race. He appeared happy but hated his job. Six years ago, Alex caught his boss who was engaged in a bribery scandal. Still, when he reported him to his superiors, they told his boss what he did instead. When we met, he told me he still remembered what his boss told him that day. 'You want to play saint, right? You will never get another promotion in the force. You will remain stuck in this position until you retire.' They never promoted him again after that. After he cried out to me, it was easy for me to flip the lid and get him on our side. We paid him and brought him in," she said.

"What about the alleged suicide deaths of the final year university students?" Ray asked.

Stella told them of Project Chameleon—which was in place before Project Hades was launched. She told them Banzida targeted the students using Lazine 520, a tasteless substance. They put it in their meals when they came to eat at Leno Palace, which drove them to chronic depression until they took their own lives.

She told them how they hacked the Kedochat accounts of their target and dropped the suicide posts before the target died.

"It was a perfect crime, and everyone believes the suicide," she said.

She told them what they already knew about TACS's illegal activities, the killings during the EndTACS protest and why Dominic and members of Banzida wanted revenge.

Ray asked the question that had been on his mind since they started interrogating Stella Odi. "Where are Dominic Tiza and Bruno Tema right now?"

CHAPTER SIXTY-THREE

Dominic Tiza tightened his fist as his mind replayed the previous day's events. Project Hades was supposed to run smoothly without a hitch. He'd made sure he gave his people everything they requested. They had conducted Project Chameleon perfectly. He'd had no doubts they would be effective in executing Project Hades.

Everything began to fall apart when they had no option but to terminate Alex Inibehe before he could talk to DSS agents. Now he knew making Alex a big part of the arrangement was a terrible mistake. The officer was a loser in his workplace who kept telling them sob stories. Now his actions had shattered their plans.

Dominic was shocked to discover they didn't have a Plan B. His men couldn't do anything else— foolish set of humans! He was working with incompetent people who also made the terrible mistake of not killing those two DSS agents.

When he saw them at the venue while watching a live feed of the event at his house in Nigeria, he knew there was a problem. Yesterday was a disaster he wanted to forget. So, he'd flown from Nigeria to his home in Freetown. Bruno had travelled with him too and put the best security detail money could buy in the compound. He didn't want to take chances. He would complete one more business deal here before he left the country and disappeared in the bowels of the Middle East and Europe, where no one would find him.

As he moved in his wheelchair, he stopped and arched his eyebrows when he heard a burst of gunfire. Who were they, and how did they find him?

***

The moment Ray alighted from the van, he ran to a wall, staying low and alert while holding his Beretta. Frank, Sarah, and other members of the joint taskforce composed of DSS agents and the Sierra Leone police officers joined him. They arrived in three vehicles. After Stella Odi confessed and gave them Dominic's location, their superiors informed the Sierra Leonean government, who provided them with all the resources they needed. Each taskforce member wore a black bulletproof vest and lapel mic.

The compound was well protected. Ray knew it would be foolish to knock on the gate and alert security operatives. Right then, they were a kilometre away from Dominic's location.

Ray saw a guard opening the gate and peering outside as they approached the house silently. The guard carried an AK 47 rifle.

Ray pulled the trigger. The silencer on the gun muffled the sound of the gunshot, maintaining their element of surprise.

The guard fell, his prone body propping the gate open.

Ray indicated for the rest of his team to wait outside and slide in through the entrance.

The stately building was majestic. Four massive pillars supported it. The front garden had a central flowerbed with an automatic sprinkler watering the flowers.

Ray spotted security cameras across the compound, which made their task difficult. Inside the premises, he kept his back flat against the wall and discovered that the place was filled with guards.

Dominic was ready for them. Time to put the first plan into action.

Electric light flooded the grounds, giving the enemy an advantage while putting Ray's team at risk.

Ray fired his weapon at the bulbs, shattering the ones he could see and plunging the place into darkness. Then, he signalled the rest of his men to enter through the gate.

One of the guards saw him, pointed his gun in his direction, and pulled the trigger. Ray dived and dodged the bullet at the last minute, and the whole compound erupted in gunfire.

The gunfire lasted an hour, with both sides losing people. When the gun battle became intense, Ray watched as four of his team members fell. Instead of ordering a retreat, he ordered them to circle the building and wallop the enemy.

As the gunfire became more intense, Ray heard a helicopter on the other side of the building. His eyes narrowed. He didn't need a seer to tell him what was happening.

"Cover me!" he said to Sarah, who stood beside him.

Sarah pulled off quick shots, and Ray ran to the other side of the building.

"Aaah!" A bullet hit him, grazing the lower side of his ribcage, slowing his movement.

He saw the shooter. Before he could pull the second shot, Ray pulled off three successive shots, blasting off his forehead.

Ray ran to the other side of the building and saw Bruno Tema pushing a man in a wheelchair towards a helipad.

Bruno saw him and pulled off three shots. Ray dived towards the ground as he dodged the bullets. The man moved fast towards the aircraft. The DSS agent aimed and pulled the trigger twice. Bruno cried out and slumped to the ground. Ray shot at the 'copter until it exploded.

He spoke via his lapel mic, and Frank and Sarah joined him.

"The gunmen have surrendered—six of them still alive," Sarah said.

"We killed thirteen of their men. Ten of our members lost their lives," Frank said in a sombre tone. His eyes widened as he stared closely at Ray. "You are bleeding. Let's—"

Ray cut Frank off, "Now is not the time."

They approached Dominic Tiza and surrounded him.

Dominic brought out his gun, but the three agents beat him to it and pointed their weapons at him.

He collapsed back in his wheelchair, his expression resigned.

"Dominic Tiza, also known as Dominic Tersoo, you are under arrest for murder and treason. We are taking you back to Nigeria, where you will answer for your crimes."

Ray handcuffed him, dragging him and six of his men who had surrendered out of the compound.

EPILOGUE

Four months later

It was a beautiful Saturday evening and the best time for a weekend getaway. Ray had used this time to embark on a weekend trip with his girlfriend, Loretta, to rekindle their relationship, which their demanding jobs had threatened.

This evening, both were relaxing at Oniru Beach on Victoria Island. Ray loved the beach because it was well kept and private. The Oniru Royal family owned the beach. It helped its clients to release the stress associated with working in their jobs.

Ray was bare-chested and wore only blue boxers while lying on a mat close to a palm tree. Loretta wore a bikini and lay beside him. The couple held each other's hands and enjoyed the gentle breeze from the palm tree.

His phone rang, and he stretched out his hand to grab it.

"No," Loretta said. She collected the phone and switched it off. "The agency gave you a break. You have worked so hard; now is time for you to rest. Let me take care of you."

Ray tried to protest but closed his mouth when her soft hands began to rub oil across his back. He closed his eyes when she massaged the stubborn muscles. Soon, all that happened over the past four months flashed across his mind.

When Dominic and his men were arrested and extradited to Nigeria, Stella released more names. The DSS and police started a nationwide manhunt that brought down Banzida criminal network. Other members of Ogid were arrested alongside forty people involved in the plot. They were sentenced to life imprisonment. In addition, the government shut down Leno's Palace and turned Esiris into a public corporation.

The DSS released two tapes Dominic gave them after verifying the source. The first tape showed EndTACS Panel of Inquiry members collecting bribes from politicians. The second tape captured the shooting of unarmed protestors by police officers during the EndTACS protest. Outrage from the masses followed the release of the recordings and made them cry out for justice.

Immediately after its release, the Inspector General of Police, Harrison Giwa, pleaded guilty to sending armed police officers to shoot at unarmed protesters and resigned from his job. The government ordered DSS to arrest him and members of EndTACS Panel of Inquiry, and they did.

After an intense court case that lasted for three months, the IGP and the End TACS Panel of Inquiry members were sentenced to twenty years each.

Ray was glad that all the guilty people paid for their crimes no matter how high they were in society. Everyone was equal before the law.

Right now, members of his team were on vacation. He'd spoken with Sarah yesterday, who was assigned to a new NIA case and was in Nairobi.

He loved her courage but felt terrible for hurting her feelings. Still, he needed to do what he did. Otherwise, they would have ended up hurting each other and becoming ineffective at their jobs.

He pushed the thoughts to the back of his mind and focused on the perfect beauty beside him. He kissed Loretta's forehead and cuddled her. "I missed you so much, honey."

"Sweetheart, I cried when I discovered you were captured. I knew Frank was lying to me. I felt that something was terribly wrong." Loretta's eyes glistened with tears.

Ray fixed his gaze on her face. "Honey, that is in the past. We have brought down Banzida. All the people behind the attacks are now in prison."

Loretta stared at him, doubt clogging her beautiful face. "Is it really in the past? Sweetheart, this job you are doing is dangerous. Why don't you quit? I won't survive if any harm comes to you."

Ray held her hands. "Honey, I can't quit. I love my job. When I fail, evil wins. But when my team and I win, the country is safer, and the criminals are kept out of the streets."

He stared into her eyes and watched her nod. He knew she understood the sacrifice he had to make. He wasn't a regular guy and didn't live a normal life.

As she stared at him, a warm smile appeared on her face. She closed the gap between them and kissed him hard. When they parted, they held each other's hands and stared at the blue sky.

The End

Thank you for reading Under The Radar by Stanley Umezulike. Please leave a review on the site of purchase.

Books in the Ray Okon series
Ties That Bind
Under The Radar

About the Author
Stanley Umezulike is an award-winning author of intriguing crime fiction novels with romantic elements set in tropical Africa. He found his passion for writing at 14 years old, and he's been writing ever since. Stanley is the creator of the popular Ray Okon series. His writing has appeared in various publications, including Daily Sun (Nigeria), Love Africa Book Club, Creative Freelance Writerz-Africa, Medium, Love Africa Press and Spillwords.

He is the founder of Prolific Fiction Writers Community on Facebook, where he helps fiction writers gain clarity and learn the art of storytelling. In addition, Stanley co-founded Ifeadigo Publishing Company Limited, a tech-driven self-publishing firm that publishes books in print and digital platforms, connects authors with global readers, and helps them shine worldwide.

In recognition of his work of transforming lives through storytelling and sharing his stories with the world, Stanley was awarded Top 40 International Leading Youth Award 2020 in the best author of the year Male Category, an initiative organized by Make Me Elegant Foundation to commemorate the

International Youth Day and celebrate youths across the world who have been truly outstanding and impactful in their various fields.

Stanley is currently working on his next book. When he's not working, he enjoys watching crime thriller TV shows, listening to good music, and travelling to new places. He lives in Awka, Nigeria. Stanley loves to hear from readers, so follow or drop him a note.

Connect with Stanley on social media:

Instagram:

https://www.instagram.com/stanley_umezulike/

Twitter:

https://www.twitter.com/stanumezulike

Facebook:

https://www.facebook.com/OfficialStanleyUmezulikel/

Goodreads:

https://www.goodreads.com/stanleyumezulike

OTHER BOOKS BY LOVE AFRICA PRESS

How To Love An Ogre by Zee Monodee
Love In The Bar by Maggie Smart
The Future King by Kiru Taye
A Small-Town Girl by Diana Anyango

CONNECT WITH US

Facebook.com/LoveAfricaPress
Twitter.com/LoveAfricaPress
Instagram.com/LoveAfricaPress

SIGN UP FOR OUR NEWSLETTER
https://www.loveafricapress.com/newsletter

LOVE AFRICA
PRESS
African Love Stories